Jingo Fever

Jingo Fever

by

Stephanie Golightly Lowden

CRICKHOLLOW BOOKS

Crickhollow Books, based in Milwaukee, Wisconsin, is an independent press working to create books of lasting quality.

Our titles are available from your favorite bookstore online or around the corner. For a complete catalog of all our titles or to place special orders (for classroom use, etc.):

www.CrickhollowBooks.com

Jingo Fever
© 2011, Stephanie Golightly Lowden

Original Trade Softcover

This is a work of fiction. The characters are drawn primarily from the imagination, and any resemblance to actual persons living or dead is coincidental.

The background image on the cover is from a postcard of Second Street in Ashland, Wisconsin, circa 1915. The image (WHi-28819) is courtesy Wisconsin Historical Society. The photograph of the seated girl sewing is also from the World War I period. The Liberty Bonds poster of 1918 ("For home and country – Victory Liberty Loan") is from the Library of Congress Prints and Photographs Division.

ISBN-13: 978-1-933987-16-3

Cover design by Philip Martin

Acknowledgements

I would like to express my gratitude to Professor E. David Cronon, who took me on as a work-study student many years ago and introduced me to the wonders of microfiche—and to the fascinating history of Wisconsin, especially Milwaukee during World War I. His research into civil-rights abuses during that World War I era opened up a whole new world of study for this undergraduate history major.

Thanks also are due to my mom, Dorothy Golightly, who lived through that same war. She inspired this book with the words: "I remember when they burned all the German language books."

Special thanks to Jamie and Katie, my continuing sources of inspiration, and to Larry, who convinced me to switch from typewriter to computer; thanks, hon.

Stephanie Golightly Lowden

*To Jamie and Katie
and Larry*

Chapter One

"Why don't you go back to Germany where you came from!"

"Yeah! Go on home, Kraut."

The boys' shouts followed Adelle as she raced toward her uncle's house on the shores of Lake Superior. She wished she could just scream at them: *I'm not from Germany, I'm from Milwaukee!*

But of course she didn't have the nerve. Why did she and her mother have to come to this awful town anyway?

Suddenly, the heel of her high button shoe caught in a rut. Adelle's dress and petticoat went flying up as she tumbled to the ground. *Ugh.* Mother's groceries flew in all directions. The spring thaw had turned the streets of Ashland to mud. As least she had long stockings on.

The hooting laughter of the boys came closer. Tears sprang to her eyes and she wished she could just disappear into the ground.

Adelle scrambled to pick up the cans of food and fresh fruit, now bruised. A can of beans rolled out of her reach.

"Quite a mess you made there, Kraut Klein," one

of the boys teased. "Hey, Howie, you like the sound of that—Kraut Klein?"

"That's perfect," the other boy answered. "Wanna' play kick the can?" He sent the canned beans spinning across the street.

Adelle crawled through the mud, frantically grabbing the remaining groceries and stuffing them back into the sack. She stood up, eyed the can that had rolled away and started walking toward it. But the boy named Howie was faster than she. Just as she bent over to pick up the can, he kicked it out of reach once again. Mortified, Adelle straightened and ran.

When she neared her uncle's house—a cabin really, by Milwaukee's standards—she slowed her pace. Even though there was a chill in the air, sweat trickled down her forehead. Adelle took a deep breath. She didn't want Mother to know those boys were picking on her because she was German. There was no telling what embarrassing thing Mother might do in response; she was so proud of her German heritage, she didn't seem to realize that it was 1918, and the United States had been at war with the Kaiser for almost a year.

Adelle admonished herself for even thinking such a thing. Mother was more concerned about the outcome of this war than anyone. Adelle's brother, Karl, had volunteered for the U.S. army against her wishes and was now somewhere in France with his division. For a brief moment Adelle imagined Karl being shot at, being hit, blood dripping down his forehead. She winced. These horrible images came to her more frequently now, since his letters had stopped coming.

Adelle took a deep breath and shook off her fear. The faint scents of cedar and pine were smothered by the odor of fish. *Yuck.* The whole town smelled of it, but Uncle Mike's house was right on Lake Superior, so the fish smell was even stronger here, especially now in the first months of summer. For some reason it bothered her more this year than before.

"You're finally home," her mother said as Adelle entered the small cabin. "What took . . . ?" Mother looked at Adelle's mud-spattered dress. "What in the world?"

"I . . . fell down." Adelle avoided her mother's eyes.

"Look at me, *Mädchen.*" Her mother drew out the German word for *girl* in a way that meant trouble. "Adelaide, tell me the truth."

Adelle had never been successful lying to her mother.

"I was running." *That much was true.*

"Running? On these muddy roads? Whatever for?"

Adelle kept silent. She couldn't lie, but she didn't want to tell the whole truth either.

"Ad-e-laide . . . I want the truth." When her mother used her full name, instead of Adelle or Addy, she knew she couldn't avoid the true explanation any longer.

"Some stupid boys. They were calling me names."

Her mother turned quickly and began putting the

groceries away with purpose. "Because you're German."
Her words sounded like a quick slap.

"I guess." She didn't want Mother to start in again on
how she must stand up for her German roots. It seemed
everybody hated them since they'd come to Ashland,
and Mother wasn't helping the situation. These days,
with the Great War on, some people thought anyone
from Milwaukee was an enemy spy. Her Uncle Mike
said it was because there were so many Germans living
in Milwaukee and a lot of them had only been in this
country a short time.

Her mother was still mad. "They're just uninformed,
foolish boys. *Dummkopfs.* Ignore them."

Adelle wished Mother wouldn't use those German
words, but she wasn't about to tell her so. Instead, she
joined her at the cupboard, helping to put things away.
"Do you really think this is the war to end all wars?"

"That's what President Wilson hopes." Her mother
sighed. "That's what we all hope." She looked at Adelle,
gray eyes sad.

She's thinking of Karl. Mother almost never spoke
about him, but Adelle knew he was on her mind all the
time. It seemed like Mother had aged since the war
began. Karl's last letter had arrived in March, but it
was June now so they didn't know where he was. All
he'd said was that his division was heading toward the
Front. The Front. The word had an ominous tone, like
some huge wave that would swallow them all.

Mother had been dead set against Karl going off to fight her homeland, but Adelle's father said that she shouldn't look at it that way. He was fighting the Kaiser—and wasn't that why their parents had left Germany not so long ago? To get away from the Kaiser's unfair laws?

Mother agreed, but she was still against the war. She didn't say much outside the family, though. A law had just been passed that said you couldn't talk against the war. Daddy said the whole country had jingo fever.

When Adelle had asked what that meant, he replied, "It's when people get overly patriotic. They do everything to prove their loyalty to America – including mean, unfair, things. They become suspicious of people they think are not like them. Right now, German-Americans are suspect simply because they or their relatives came from Germany at some time in the past

He shook his head. "It's ridiculous."

Remembering the conversation made her miss Father all the more. He always had time for her questions and explained things so clearly. Mother didn't want to talk about the war, or, it seemed, anything else these days.

War, war, war . . . and the different ways people reacted to it. It was all so confusing for Adelle. But she knew one thing: she was afraid for Karl. The image of him being shot returned.

She squeezed her eyes shut and forced herself to think of something pleasant. Anything.

Ice cream. That would taste good right now. She was still warm from running.

"How's Uncle Mike?" she asked, eager to change the subject.

"About the same."

"I still don't see why he can't just move to Milwaukee, and we could all stay together there."

"Now, Adelle, we've been all through that. This is Mike's home. He'd be miserable in a big city."

"Well, I'm miserable here," Adelle burst out.

Mother looked stung. "Don't you use that tone with me, young lady. Go clean yourself up."

Adelle stalked off to the room she shared with her mother. She closed the door and took off her dress. There was mud on the hem and a few splotches here and there, but her petticoat and stockings had taken the worst of it. *Stupid boys.* If only she had the nerve to stand up to them.

Her thoughts were interrupted by a knock on the door. "Adelle?"

"Just a minute." She slipped a clean petticoat and dress over her head. No stockings—she was still too hot.

Mother stood in the doorway. "I'm going to town for a few things. You keep an eye on Uncle Mike. Get him anything he needs."

"What are you going to town for? I was just there."

"You forgot the can of beans."

Adelle looked away. In her mind's eye she saw that boy kicking the can, hard, just as she was about to pick it up. "Oh, sorry."

She followed her mother into the small room that served as kitchen and sitting area. She watched her leave, and noticed that her mother did not immediately head toward town. Instead, Adelle's mother walked to the lakefront and just stood there, looking out at the waters as the small waves quietly rippled onto the sandy shore. Standing there, so close to the lake, Adelle suddenly thought her mother looked vulnerable, as if the mighty lake might sweep her away.

"She sure does love that lake."

Adelle whirled around, startled by her uncle's voice. "Uncle Mike, I thought you were sleeping."

"A man can only stand so much sleep, Addy."

Uncle Mike had called her Addy for as long as she could remember. Now, it reminded her of happier times shared with him, when there wasn't so much to worry about.

She pulled out a kitchen chair. "Here, Uncle, sit down and I'll make you some tea." She filled the kettle, put it on the stove, and spooned out the tea into the infuser. She placed it carefully into her uncle's old, chipped teapot and set a china cup and saucer in front of him.

"You're growing up to be quite the lady." Uncle Mike smiled at her.

Adelle couldn't help but notice how much older he

looked this year. He'd taken sick over the winter. That was why she and her mother planned to spend the whole summer up here, instead of their usual month.

"Thank you, Uncle Mike."

"So, how are you enjoying your first week in the wilds of the north?"

"Well," Adelle sat down across from him, not sure how to tell him that this year, more than ever, she missed Milwaukee.

He smiled knowingly. "I know, you're a city girl. Of course, for these parts, Ashland is considered a city." He laughed.

Adelle had to chuckle, too. "A very tiny little city."

There were not enough big buildings, and too many trees everywhere for her taste. She frowned, just thinking about how dark it was here at night. *Why did it bother her so much? It never had before.*

"Don't look so glum, child. There's things to do here. Not as many as in Milwaukee, I suppose. Tell me, what would you be doing if you were home now?"

"Well, summer vacation just started, so I'd be helping Father in the grocery store." Adelle loved that store, where a creaky ceiling fan swirled the mixed scents of fresh vegetables, pipe tobacco and new cloth all around her. Here in Ashland, there was nothing but woods and lake and the ever-present smell of fish.

"You're day-dreaming."

"Sorry." *How long had she been staring into space?*

"I . . . was just thinking about Father and the store."

"I am sorry you got stuck coming up here to take care of your ailing bachelor uncle. That influenza sure did take its toll." His eyes grew sad.

Adelle knew Uncle Mike's fishing partner, a fellow named Steven Byers, had died earlier that year of the bad flu that had spread quickly and taken the whole country in its grip. "I'm sorry, Uncle Mike."

"Thank you, child. It was a bad spring." Suddenly, he was overtaken by a spasm of coughing.

The kettle answered with a steady shriek.

Adelle jumped up. "Just in time. This will settle your lungs." She poured the boiling water over the tea infuser.

"What's left of my lungs," he said, as his shaky hand reached for the teapot.

"Let it steep a few minutes." Adelle gazed out the big window at Lake Superior. She didn't want him to talk too much, afraid that would bring on another spasm. Uncle Mike's flu had turned into pneumonia. He was on the mend now, but he almost died.

"So," Uncle Mike began, his voice as rough as tree bark, "you're not as fond of our great lake up north as your mother is."

The first night, just a week ago when Adelle and her mother had arrived in Ashland, Mother had taken her daughter out to "enjoy the view." This was her family's tradition. Every year when they first arrived, they would run right to the edge of the lake. Adelle hadn't minded in the past, but this year, it seemed bigger and blacker somehow. Almost threatening.

"I don't know, Uncle Mike. There's something . . . scary about it."

Uncle Mike nodded as he sipped his hot tea. "Well, there can be. That's for sure. Every fisherman learns not to take this lake for granted. It can yield up a wealth of fish, or it can swallow you whole in a storm quicker than you can say jack rabbit. It's not particular and shows no favorites. You have to respect it."

"I guess. I just think . . . Lake Michigan in Milwaukee is different."

"How so?"

"Well, this time of year, it's a place to swim and have picnics with friends. There's even a place to get ice cream across from our favorite beach."

She thought of last summer, before her brother Karl went away. They went to the beach with some friends and splashed in Lake Michigan. Karl dunked her but didn't hold her down long; he knew when to stop teasing. Soon they were covered with goose bumps and, after warming up on the hot sand, they got ice cream from the vendor and ate it until their lips turned blue.

"Well, now, child," said Uncle Mike, "we have picnics here too. But if you think Lake Michigan is any safer than Superior, you are mistaken. These Great Lakes are all fickle maidens. Kind to you one minute, savage the next."

Fishing sounded to Adelle like a dangerous job. "How come you like it up here so much then?"

He lifted the teapot and filled his cup. "It's like the sea, child. So like the sea."

"Lake Superior?"

"Yes."

"Have you actually been on the ocean?"

"Oh, yes. I was nine years old when we came to America. I remember the crossing like it was yesterday."

"Really? Was it fun?"

"For me, yes. Not sure all the other passengers in steerage would agree with me though." He laughed, and the laugh made his cough start up again.

Adelle patted him on the back. "What's steerage?"

She shouldn't have asked. Talking was hard for her uncle. "Never mind. You should be still." She poured him more tea.

"I'm fine. Don't fuss." He cleared his throat. "Steerage is how most of us came to America. No fancy cabins. Everybody all together in the belly of the ship. The women, it was hardest on them. They'd put up curtains around the small area their family claimed, to get some privacy. Oh, how they complained of the stench!"

"You mean the ship smelled bad?"

"Oh, Liebchen, did it ever. There were a lot of people crowded together, eating, getting sea-sick . . . you get the idea."

"Yuck." Adelle didn't want to even imagine it.

"But for a boy of nine, it was an adventure. I didn't mind the rocking of the boat. Took to it like an old sailor. For two months, I was in my glory."

Uncle Mike was looking out at the lake, but Adelle suspected he was seeing the Atlantic.

"Standing on deck, sea spray in my face, I vowed I'd be a sailor on the Seven Seas when I grew up."

"Were you ever?"

"The Almighty had a different plan for me. But I found the next best thing to sailing the ocean. Living here, fishing this Great Lake."

Adelle didn't know these things about her uncle. He'd always been busy out fishing the other years they'd visited. He didn't have a lot of time to sit and tell stories.

"Your mother was twelve when we crossed the Atlantic," he continued. "She loved the homeland dearly and didn't want to leave her girl friends in Germany. She was angry, those first years in Milwaukee. Once our folks got settled and had a little money to spare, your grandparents brought us kids up here on holiday one year. She must have been about sixteen."

He chuckled softly. "She met a boyfriend here that summer. Your father. I think that's why she's always loved the lake—it reminds her of that special time when she first met your dad. Since then, it's always cheered her to come up here. She never even minded the chill of the lake."

So, there was a time when her mother was angry to have to leave her friends too. But leaving them behind in Germany—she must have known she'd never see them again. Adelle felt guilty for feeling sorry for herself, stuck up here without her friends but just for a short time. At least she would be going back to Milwaukee eventually.

And eventually, Mother had learned to love this part of the world. It was hard for Adelle to picture her mother a young girl, in love. She knew Mother and Father had met here and that Father eventually moved to Milwaukee where there were more opportunities. That was about all Adelle had known. Until now.

Still, she was an outsider here in Ashland. Would she ever learn to love this place like her mother did? "I just wish . . ." How could she explain to Uncle Mike that she felt like an alien here? Someone who just didn't belong.

Uncle Mike was silent for a long time. Then he took a sip of tea. "It's the times, Addy. After the war people will get their senses back."

So, he must have heard her telling Mother about those stupid boys. His eyes looked sad, and a wave of empathy rippled through her. Uncle Mike had not only lost his friend, but his business partner as well. And from conversations Adelle had overheard between her parents, it was clear Uncle Mike was having money problems. Now with his poor health he couldn't even go fishing—the thing he loved most, and his livelihood.

She spotted her mother coming up the walk. Time passed quickly for Adelle when she was talking with her uncle. If he would only move back to Milwaukee, she could hear more of his stories.

"So, how's the patient doing?" Mother hurried in with one small package. Adelle had almost forgotten about the incident with the beans.

"I'm just fine, big sister. Having an enjoyable conversation with this lovely young lady."

Adelle smiled at him appreciatively but got up to leave. Now that Mother was home she thought she'd sneak away to the bedroom and pick up where she'd left off in the novel she was reading, *Twenty Thousand Leagues Under the Sea*. Professor Aronnax had just fallen into the sea when she'd last put the book down.

Mother looked from Uncle Mike to Adelle. "She is growing up, isn't she?" There was that sadness in her voice again.

Then she cleared her throat and put on her stoic front once again. "I see you made some tea. Is it helping, Mike?"

"It's helping just fine. She's a good girl, Emma."

Adelle felt her face flush as she excused herself and headed for the bedroom.

"Oh, Adelle, wait. While I was in town I noticed a flyer advertising an ice cream social on Sunday. I thought you might like to go."

Sunday was tomorrow.

"Who would I go with?" The one friend she had seen up here every year before this one, Clara, had moved away. To Minnesota, they said, to be with family. Adelle and Clara had been childhood "holiday friends" since they were little.

And surely Mother would have to stay here with Uncle Mike.

"I think we should all go," said Mother, to Adelle's surprise. "The fresh air would do Mike good."

"That it would," Mike agreed.

Adelle's stomach tightened. What if they went and people shunned them because they were German? What if those awful boys were there?

"I don't think I want to go." Adelle quickly stepped from the main room and hurried into the sanctuary of the bedroom, shutting the door behind her.

"*Liebchen?*" Mother was at the door.

"Come in," Adelle sighed.

Her mother slipped in, closing the door behind her. "I know how you love ice cream."

Adelle didn't answer.

"Uncle Mike's friend, Steven . . . his family are up here. We can go to the social with them. I'm sure they're decent people."

Adelle had never met them. The family of Uncle Mike's lost fishing partner had always been gone on holiday the other years Adelle had been here. Steven's sister, Adelle had heard, was married to a doctor, with enough money to allow the family to spend summers out East.

"I don't know, Mother. The people up here – this year, they don't like Germans." Adelle tried not to talk back, even though she felt like arguing.

"That's just a few silly, ignorant boys. It's time you made some friends, since we're going to be up here all summer." Her mother's voice held that tone that meant the discussion was over. She left the room.

Adelle bit her lower lip. If it were just a few silly boys that didn't like Germans, why did so many people stare at them when they went to town? She'd even heard a woman whisper at the general store about "those Germans." How could she ever make friends here again?

Adelle flopped down on the bed. *Ugh,* she wanted to cry out. This was turning into the worst summer ever. She should be in Milwaukee with her friends instead of stuck here in the middle of nowhere, being picked on by stupid boys and smelling fish all the day and night. And now this.

But she knew there was no getting out of it. Her mother's mind was made up. They were going to the ice cream social.

Chapter Two

Sunday dawned foggy with a slight drizzle. Adelle looked out the bedroom window and smiled. They couldn't go to the ice cream social in the rain.

She got out of bed, slipped off her nightgown, and took her Sunday dress out of the small, musty-smelling closet. She shivered. Even her dress smelled like a mixture of fish and moldy socks. There was nothing to be done about it, though. Even if they skipped the ice cream social, they were going to church today for the first time since arriving, and she had to dress properly.

She emerged from the bedroom to the smell of bacon cooking and inhaled deeply. That was better. Maybe this wouldn't be such a bad day after all. After church Adelle could read her book all day.

"I guess we can't go to the park in the rain." She slid into her chair.

"We'll see," Mother answered.

"The damp air would be bad for Uncle Mike, wouldn't it?" Adelle was glad this excuse had just popped into her head at the right time.

"The weather might clear. It's early. The social doesn't start until two o'clock. We'll let Uncle Mike rest at home while we go to church."

Adelle ate her breakfast in silence, mentally crossing her fingers in hopes that the weather wouldn't clear.

Later, at the Catholic mass, when the priest talked about the Great War, Adelle's thoughts shifted to her brother Karl. *Please God, keep him safe. We haven't had a letter from him in so long I'm worried. I keep seeing these horrible things in my mind. Things that might have happened to him. Please don't let him be hurt or worse.* And then the scene that had replayed so many times in her mind intruded on her prayer: Karl being shot. Karl bleeding, suffering, dying. She squeezed her eyes shut and willed the thought away.

When they came out of church, the sun was shining brightly, but Adelle didn't feel the warmth. She was still chilled from her haunting thoughts about Karl.

"It looks like it will be a nice day after all," Mother commented as they walked away from the church and headed toward the house.

"It'll still be muddy at the park though, won't it?" Adelle asked hopefully.

"There's plenty of time for the sun to do its work."

By two o'clock, the sun was still out, and all three of them were off to the park. As they walked, Uncle Mike had a spring to his step Adelle hadn't seen since they'd arrived in Ashland.

"It'll be good seeing Elizabeth and her family again. I haven't seen them since before Steven and I took sick."

Although Uncle Mike smiled, his voice had a tinge of sadness, and Adelle felt a wave of sorrow grip her heart. It must be dreadful to lose someone you love. Like Karl. She shook herself, trying to chase away the demons of fear, but it didn't help much.

"Cold, Addy?" Uncle Mike put an arm around her.

"Just a little, I guess."

Her mother's cheery voice broke the dark spell. "I'm anxious to meet your friends, Mike. How old are Elizabeth's children?"

Didn't Mother ever think of Karl? Wasn't she thinking about him right now, like Adelle was? Mother never even mentioned his name anymore. It was as if he were already . . .

"Let's see now, Joey Johnson went off to war, after just finishing college. Agnes must be going on eighteen, and the little one—Nora—she must be about Addy's age."

"Hear that, Adelle? You'll have someone new to spend time with today."

Adelle cleared her mind of dark thoughts and tried to focus on the social. It would be nice if she could make a new friend or two up here. Especially since Clara moved away. At least it didn't sound like there were any creepy boys in Elizabeth's family to tease her about being German. Maybe today would be fun after all.

By the time they got to the park, the sun and a warm breeze had burned off all the dampness, just like her mother thought it would. People gathered in small groups, some of them already sitting on the lawn, others clustered around the table where the ice cream was being served. The park, right on Chequamegon Bay, reminded her of her favorite beach at home in Milwaukee. A hollow, homesick feeling settled in Adelle's stomach.

A woman from one of the groups smiled and waved. "Mike, it's so good to see you out and about," she said as she came over to greet them. "This must be your family." The woman paused and her kind eyes took in Adelle and her mother.

"I'm Elizabeth Byers Johnson. Steven was my brother."

"Oh, I'm so sorry," Adelle's mother said, and the two women talked in low voices as Mrs. Johnson led them back to her family. Once there, introductions were made all over again. Elizabeth's husband was a doctor practicing in the war, so she and her daughters were living alone for now. Nora, the youngest, with long, blond braids, smiled at her. But when Adelle met the eyes of the older girl, Agnes, all she got was a cold stare. Adelle wondered what she could have done to offend her.

As the two older women fussed over Uncle Mike, young Nora approached Adelle. "Hi."

"Hi."

"So—you want to get some ice cream?" Nora asked.

"Sure." Adelle could never turn down ice cream, and this girl seemed nice enough.

As they headed to the ice cream table, Adelle looked

over the crowd, trying to determine if they were staring at her or not. Several glanced up from their blanket seats, but most were busy talking to friends or licking ice cream. Adelle ordered a triple-dip strawberry cone, and Nora got chocolate. The cones were so tall they almost toppled over on the way back to Adelle's blanket.

"Let's not sit too close to the grown-ups," Nora whispered as she motioned for Adelle to help her move the blanket. "They'll just be talking about the war."

Adelle was relieved. "That's all anybody talks about anymore."

Nora seemed to study Adelle for a moment. "I thought you'd have a German accent. Your Uncle Mike does."

Adelle felt her face go hot. "He was born in Germany. So was my mother, but we all speak English at home. My parents insist on it."

"So you don't speak German at all?"

"I know a few words." Actually, she knew more than a few. She knew how to speak German almost as good as her mother.

Nora licked away an ice cream trail running down the side of her cone. "I'm learning French from my mother."

"Really? Is she French?"

"Oh, no, English. Father is Swedish. But mother's mother—my grandma back East—thinks every young lady should learn French—that it's the language of the well bred." Nora giggled.

Adelle smiled back. "I guess I'll be taking Latin in

high school, but that's two years away." She wasn't about to tell Nora that, in a moment of war-fueled patriotism, the principal at her school had ordered all of the German language books removed from the library. She'd heard rumors that the offending books had been burned.

She had imagined the pile of books, volumes of poetry by Goethe and Schiller, works of philosophy and science, smoldering, then bursting into flames.

It wasn't just the books, though. Since the war started, German-Americans out in public places spoke their native language at their peril.

Adelle noticed Nora's attention shift to the park entrance. Adelle squinted, but all she could make out was a group of young people entering. Maybe they were friends of Nora's. Then, as they moved closer, Adelle realized who two of them were—the boys who teased her yesterday.

"Do you know them?" Adelle asked. The bit of cone she'd just eaten stuck in her throat.

Nora blushed. "Yes. They're in my class at school." She sat up straight and quickly licked the drips from the side of her cone.

The way Nora was looking at them, Adelle had the feeling the boys were either friends of hers or she wished they were. Adelle bit her lower lip. What would she do if they came over? With her head down, Adelle watched the boys, waiting to see if they saw Nora.

At first they just stood there, eyeing the crowd. Then,

they spotted the two girls on the blanket.

Two of the boys started elbowing one of them, as if teasing. They pushed him, playfully, toward Nora's family.

As he came closer, Adelle recognized Howard—the one who'd kicked her "missing" can of beans down the street. She looked away, wishing she had the nerve to tell him what she thought of him. Instead, she turned around so her back would be to him as he approached.

"Hi," she heard the other boy say to Nora.

"Hello, Arthur," Nora answered. "I'd like you to meet my friend . . ."

She had no choice now. Adelle had to turn around.

"Adelle, this is Arthur. He's a friend in my class." Nora's face seemed lit from within when she smiled at him.

Maybe she could simply concentrate on her ice cream and not even look at him. But then Adelle thought of the can of beans rolling down the street, and she prickled with renewed anger. She took a deep breath and forced herself to look up at Arthur.

"We've met." She wouldn't even look at Howard.

"Uh, hello," Arthur stammered. Adelle realized he had just now figured out who she was. He blushed and turned away.

"You've met?" Nora looked from Adelle to Arthur. "When?"

"I have to go," was Arthur's only reply, and he quickly

disappeared with his friends into the crowd.

Nora looked stricken. "What was all that about?"

Adelle finished her cone before answering. She didn't know this girl, but she would really like to have a friend while she was stuck up here all summer. If she told her what she thought of Arthur, Nora might get mad.

Still, she felt she had to explain what had happened.

"Arthur, and that one friend of his . . ." Adelle pointed to the boy whose name she knew was Howard.

"Howard?"

"That's the one. I was walking home from the grocery store and slipped on the mud. The two of them kicked my groceries all over the street."

"What?"

"Really. They did."

"Well, they are pretty mischievous. They get into trouble sometimes in school, but nothing really bad. I wonder why they would do that to you."

"I don't think they like Germans."

"That's dumb. Did they say that?"

"Somehow they knew who I was. They called me Kraut Klein."

"Well, in this town, everybody knows who everybody is. Did you meet them before, in past years when you came up here?"

"No. We never stayed very long before. I had one friend—a girl named Clara. She moved away."

"Everyone I know is fond of your Uncle Mike. I don't see why Arthur and Howard would do that."

"My mother says they are just uninformed boys."

"Give them another chance. This war has made everyone crazy. They can be really sweet. Especially Arthur." Nora got a dreamy look on her face.

Sweet? Adelle doubted that.

Although—if that Howard boy wasn't such a jerk, he'd actually be kind of cute.

Just then she noticed Nora's older sister get up and leave the group of grown-ups. Nora noticed too.

"Agnes, where are you going?" Nora called out, but the young woman didn't answer. Nora jumped up and made a move to follow her, but her mother shook her head, and Nora sat back down on the blanket.

"She must have one of her headaches again." Nora sighed.

"Is she ill?" Adelle thought that might account for the girl's rude behavior.

"Mother says she's sick at heart. Her fiancé was killed in some awful battle in France. She's been having headaches ever since she found out."

Adelle's heart raced. *An awful battle in France.* "When did you find out? " She could hear the shrill panic in her own voice.

Nora looked at her, startled. "They got the telegram about three weeks ago. Why?"

"My brother, Karl, he's over there on the front lines,

too. We haven't heard from him since March." Adelle got up. She had to tell Mother this new information.

"Oh, I'm sure he's okay. If he were killed, the government would have let you know by now. I mean, if he died in the same battle as Mark, that was Agnes' boyfriend, you'd have a telegram, Adelle."

Adelle sat back down. She was shaking all over. "I just get so worried when we don't hear from my brother."

Tears started, but she brushed them away.

Nora finished the last of her cone. "I'm so sick of this war. I wish Father were here. He's a doctor, you know, so he's mostly behind the lines, working in the field hospitals. It sounds terrible, all the poor boys . . . "

The girl lay down on her back, shielding her eyes from the sun, and looked at Nora. "Is your father off at war too?"

Wasn't it enough that her brother was in France getting shot at? "No, he's in Milwaukee running our grocery store."

Adelle lay down on the blanket beside Nora. The grass smelled clean and new, the way it does after a rain. She inhaled its perfume deeply. "Let's not talk about the stupid war. I'm tired of it." She closed her eyes as her heartbeat slowed to normal.

"Good idea," Nora sighed. "Tell me about Milwaukee. I mean, it must be big and exciting. Like New York, right?'

"Well, it's bigger than Ashland. But I doubt it's like

New York." Adelle didn't want to tell Nora she thought Ashland was the most boring place she'd ever been. But she'd never thought that before. Why was this year so different? Mother said it was because she was older and no longer found the amusements of childhood interesting. But Adelle wondered if it was the war—painting everything with an ugly hue.

"So—what do you do for fun in Milwaukee?" Nora asked.

"We have a lot of theatres, with plays and moving pictures both."

"We have three picture shows in Ashland."

"Really? I didn't know that. We never went to one up here." Maybe there would be fun things to do here after all. "We used to go to the Pabst Theatre in Milwaukee a lot. It's a very fancy theater, where they put on plays. But then . . ." *Should she tell Nora what happened there?*

"But then what?"

"They used to put on a lot of German language plays there. But since the war, that became too unpopular. Someone even set up a machine gun across the street from the theatre, just to keep people from going to the German plays."

"A machine gun? Really? That's strange. Isn't Milwaukee mostly German people? How could that happen there?"

"There are a lot of German-Americans in Milwaukee, but not everyone. My parents say the war is causing problems for many different people, for anyone who is against the war. And not just in Milwaukee."

"How did we get on this boring subject again?" Nora asked. "Let's talk about the movies."

"Good idea."

"Have you seen *Rebecca of Sunnybrook Farm*? I just love Mary Pickford."

Adelle sat up, eager to change the subject, and nodded vigorously. "Isn't she gorgeous? I saw it with some friends the first week it came out."

"Once," recalled Nora, "we went to Milwaukee at Christmas time. I was very young, but I remember looking at all the lovely window displays. But since Father has been gone . . ." Nora sighed. "Do most Germans in Milwaukee support the Kaiser?"

Adelle's chest tightened with anger. "Heavens, no. I don't know anybody in Milwaukee who does. It's just that a lot of people, not just German-Americans, didn't support the war at first. They didn't want America to get involved in a European war. Father says even President Wilson didn't want to get involved."

"I didn't know that. I don't keep up with news."

Adelle flopped back down on the blanket. "I thought we weren't going to talk about the war anymore."

"It just always seems to come up." Nora lay back on the blanket, head resting on her hands. "Do you have a boyfriend?"

Adelle relaxed. "Not really. But I do have friends in Milwaukee who are boys."

Nora giggled. "I think Arthur is just peachy."

Hadn't Nora heard a thing Adelle told her about him?

She went on. "He's so funny in class, he drives our teacher crazy."

"I'll bet he does." Adelle's voice held a note of sarcasm.

"Oh, he's not so bad."

Adelle shifted uneasily on the blanket and not because the damp ground was seeping through. Her anger was bubbling up again, but she didn't want to alienate her only chance at friendship this summer.

"Can you see if he's still around?" Nora asked.

Adelle leaned up on one elbow and glanced around the park quickly, recognizing no one.

"Do you see him?" Nora persisted.

"Not from here."

"Could you stand up and see if you can. Please? I don't want him to think I'm looking for him."

Reluctantly, Adelle stood up. Why was she doing this? She didn't want to find that creep. Shielding her eyes from the sun, she squinted into the distance. How many people were staring at her, the outsider? She told herself not to care, it didn't matter what people thought.

Then, she spotted Arthur, way over at the opposite end of the park.

"I can see him. He's with a bunch of people—grown-ups and kids both."

"Probably his family." Nora sat up. "Want to take a walk?" She smiled mischievously.

Adelle knew what Nora had in mind. Why did she have to be sweet on Arthur? Her stomach churned, but she knew what her answer must be. "No, thank you."

"Aw, come on. I don't want to go over there alone."

Think fast. She really should go with her and tell off Howard. But she didn't have the nerve and besides, she didn't want Nora to think she was a spoil-sport.

"I . . . I think I ate too much ice cream. I'm going to be sick." Adelle dashed off, leaving Nora with a surprised look on her face.

Chapter Three

Adelle told her mother that her stomach was a little queasy—too much ice cream—and went home. There was no point staying at the park, hanging around the adults and getting bored. It was obvious Nora preferred Arthur's company. Besides, having the house to herself would be a pleasant change. She was used to having a lot more space in her home in Milwaukee.

When she returned to the cottage, the first thing she did was put on water for tea. She'd find that book she'd been reading and escape to the world under the sea.

But she'd only read one chapter when she heard the door slam, followed by her uncle's harsh coughing.

"Uncle Mike," she said as she got up off the old worn couch. "Are you okay?"

"I might ask you the same." He looked at her, eyes squinting, as if trying to figure her out.

She avoided his gaze. "Oh, I'm fine. Just too much ice cream. Would you like some tea?"

"Surely, that would hit the spot."

"Where's Mother?"

"Oh, she and Elizabeth got on so famously that I told her to stay and have a good time. I was getting a little tired." He coughed again, this time even harder, as he slumped into the chair.

"Here, this will fix you up. Then you can take a nap." Adelle poured the tea.

"I'm tired of naps." He looked out the window wistfully.

"You could come live with us in Milwaukee. We have a lake there too, you know." Adelle had never had the nerve to actually bring up this subject with him, but after today she was more anxious than ever to get home.

"Oh, Addy, the city's no place for the likes of me. I'd miss the smell of fish."

"Uncle Mike!" Addy laughed. "Yuck. But you know we have that smell in Milwaukee too."

He smiled weakly. "That I remember, child. I once lived there."

"How long ago was that?" Adelle settled in at the table and poured herself a cup of tea. She could listen to Uncle Mike's stories all day.

"I moved here when I was eighteen. Like your mother, I'd grown fond of Lake Superior on our holiday trips up here. Never did like the city. Met Steven, he had a boat and was looking for a partner, and so we took up our fishing business soon after. Didn't make much of a living at first, but after a few years, the lake paid us back just fine."

"You miss your friend." The words were out before Adelle thought about them. She shouldn't have said it out loud like that. She didn't want him to feel bad. "I'm sorry, Uncle Mike, it's not my place."

Uncle Mike patted her hand. "Of course it's your place. I think about him every day. You saying it out loud won't make me feel bad. In fact, child, when a close friend or a loved one dies, you want people to talk about him. Otherwise it's like he never existed."

When a loved one dies. The words rang in her ears like a fire wagon's bell. *Karl? Where was he?*

"You're lookin' mighty pensive there. Penny for your thoughts?"

Adelle hesitated, then blurted it out.

"Oh, Uncle Mike! I was thinking about Karl. I can't get these terrible things out of my mind . . . about what might happen to him. Nora told me her sister's fiancé was killed about three weeks ago in France. I'm afraid Karl was in the same battle. Mother never mentions Karl anymore . . ." Adelle felt as if her lungs were swimming in water. She couldn't breathe.

"Your father would let you know if he hears anything, Addy." He kept holding her hand.

Adelle coughed and took a deep breath. "I know, but why doesn't Mother ever mention Karl? It's like he's . . . dead already." There, she said it.

"I only know . . . your brother hurt your mother by his decision to go off to war. She was dead set against him enlisting in the U.S. army and going off to fight. 'It's not our war,' she kept saying. But Karl didn't agree. 'America has chosen to get involved, and I feel I need to do my part for my country,' he told her."

Uncle Mike sighed. "Your mother can't bear to talk about him because she's so afraid she's going to lose him. He's her only son, just like you're her only daughter. She couldn't bear to lose either of you."

Adelle remembered the arguments when Karl announced he was going to war. Mother pleaded with him to come up here, help Uncle Mike with his fishing business. Karl loved to fish.

Oh, why couldn't he have done that? Adelle realized for the first time that she wasn't just worried about Karl, but she was angry with him as well.

The room was silent. Both she and Uncle Mike were lost in thought, sipping tea. Adelle heard only the chirping of birds outside the window.

"You could talk to her about Karl."

Uncle Mike looked up from his tea.

"Me? Bring up Karl?" He paused, then slowly shook his head "I don't think so. Your mother . . . she has her own battle to fight, inside. About how she feels about Karl's decision to enlist."

At first, when Karl went off to war, Mother seemed as fragile as fine crystal—crystal that might shatter if struck by the wrong words. Adelle was kind, trying not to upset her.

Then, Mother grew more strict, putting more restrictions on where Adelle could go, what she could do.

Mother talked less, and when she did it was with either a voice of disapproval or anger. She avoided talking about the war, even with Father.

Lately, Mother's behavior made Adelle just plain mad. Adelle just wanted things to be the way they used to be. But that couldn't happen until the war was over and Karl back home.

And if something happened to Karl, none of them would ever be the same again.

"There you are, Adelle. Are you all right?" Mother swooshed into the house and looked from Adelle to Mike.

"Addy and I are both fine, Emma. You should have stayed longer and visited with Elizabeth."

"With the two of you under the weather?" Mother glanced at Adelle. "What happened to you?"

Adelle picked her book up off the couch. "I guess a triple dip was a bit too much ice cream."

Mother could always tell when Adelle was lying, so Adelle just looked at Uncle Mike. "Would you like more tea, Uncle?"

But her mother came straight over. She placed her palms on Adelle's cheeks and studied her daughter's face. "Hmmm. You look well enough. Your color is good."

Adelle tried not to look her mother in the eye.

"Nora seems like a nice girl." Mother said it as if she were thinking of something else. She poured herself a cup of tea.

"Um, yeah, she's okay." Adelle glanced at Uncle Mike.

He frowned. "My goodness. You don't sound too interested."

"No, she's all right, I guess. It's just her choice of friends."

"Oh?" Uncle Mike looked intrigued.

"She likes this boy who teased me the other day about being German." Adelle glanced at her mother, who was busy heating up more water. "Nora chose to spend the afternoon with him instead of me."

"So, this is what brought on the sour stomach." Uncle Mike looked at her with understanding . . . and curiosity. "What's the boy's name?"

"Arthur. Why?"

"Oh, nothing really. I thought it might be Howard."

"That's his friend."

"Indeed?"

"Do you know them?"

"I know Mr. Billington, Howard's father. He's the grocer." Uncle Mike shook himself as if ridding himself of fleas.

"A friend of yours?" Somehow, though, Adelle doubted that by the look on her uncle's face.

"No." His tone was stern, which was quite unusual. Especially with Adelle. "It's just that . . . children can be cruel."

He seemed to want to change the subject.

"You think that's all it is? I think being German is just a bad thing to be right now."

"Well, now, Addy, I wouldn't say that. Children hear their parents say things and they repeat them." Uncle Mike's brisk tone warned Adelle not to question him further.

Adelle sat down on the couch and opened her book. "Well, I am an American. Not a German. And they are stupid boys."

Uncle Mike laughed, his dark mood passed, but Mother interrupted. "They are stupid boys, perhaps. And yes, you are American. But don't ever forget your German roots. They are an important part of you, too."

Why did Mother's ears have to perk up just then? Adelle said nothing and flopped down on the couch, hoping that was the end of her mother's lecture.

After a few moments passed, Adelle opened her book and began to read the next chapter of her adventure novel. Professor Aronnax had just been drugged and imprisoned. She lost herself to the story.

In the book, Professor Aronnax soon encounters the mysterious Captain Nemo, an eccentric fellow who commands a never-before-seen invention, a submarine, which allows him to travel around the world underwater. Nemo loves his life below the surface.

"The sea is the be all and end all! It covers seven-
tenths of the planet earth. Its breath is clean and

healthy. It's an immense wilderness where a man is never lonely, because he feels life astir on every side.

"The sea is simply movement and love; it's living infinity, as one of your poets put it, a vast pool of nature. Our globe began with the sea, so to speak, and who can say we won't end with it!

"Here lies supreme tranquility. The sea doesn't belong to tyrants. On its surface they can still exercise their iniquitous claims, battle each other, devour each other, haul every earthly horror.

"But thirty feet below sea level, their dominion ceases, their influence fades, their power vanishes!

"Ah, sir, live! Live in the heart of the seas! Here alone lies independence! Here I recognize no superiors!

Here I'm free!"

Adelle liked the sound of that.

Chapter Four

The following week was routine, until Thursday. Adelle was hanging out laundry when her mother returned from a visit to town.

"*Liebchen,*" she called.

Adelle cringed. She wished Mother wouldn't use those German words so loudly.

"I just saw Elizabeth Johnson and her daughter Nora in town. They're taking the ferry over to Madeline Island on Saturday and she invited us along. I told her we'd be thrilled to go. It will be so good for Mike."

Her mother's face was lit with enthusiasm. Madeline Island was a popular tourist spot, not far from Ashland.

"Do I have to go?" Adelle riffled through the laundry basket, looking for another blouse or shirt to hang.

"Of course you're going. Why wouldn't you want to?" Mother's eagerness quickly turned to disappointment.

Adelle immediately felt guilty. Why was she so moody? "I was just thinking, maybe Nora's creepy friends might be there."

Her mother just stared at her for a moment, uncomprehending. "You mean those boys who teased you? I don't know, but I doubt that Elizabeth invited them along. If they're there, just ignore them." Mother went on hanging clothes.

Adelle squeezed the clothespins until her fingers ached. Mother could make her go on this trip, but she could never make her happy about being German.

A cool wind, laced with spray, blew through Adelle's hair as she stood on the deck of the Madeline Island ferry. The day was warm, but out here on Lake Superior she needed her sweater. People leaned on the railings of the boat, chatting excitedly. Looking out over the massive lake, and remembering what Uncle Mike had said about not taking this lake for granted, Adelle held tightly to the railing. She glanced around the deck, wondering what or who could save her if she were suddenly pitched overboard.

"I hope you're feeling better." Nora leaned over the railing.

It took a moment for Adelle to remember the ruse she had used to leave the ice cream social. "Oh, yes. I'm fine. Just a bit too much ice cream." Adelle glanced at her mother standing nearby, but she hadn't heard.

"Don't you just love it out here?" Nora asked.

"It's a little scary, don't you think?" Adelle pulled her sweater tightly around her.

"For a city girl," Adelle's mother added, smiling into the wind.

Adelle could see that her mother was enjoying herself. Well, she would try to enjoy the day as well. Neither Arthur nor Howard were present, and the people on the ferry were all in high spirits, ready for a day away from work and worries about the war.

The only disappointment was that Uncle Mike hadn't come along. "When I get back on a boat, it'll be to fish," he'd said, standing at the cottage window and looking out at the lake. Even Mother couldn't budge him, but he insisted they go ahead and have a good time.

The lake and sky blended as one in the sunshine, and Adelle had to admit it was a dazzling sight. She couldn't help feeling, though, that the sheer uncontrolled wildness of it all might swallow her up at any moment.

"There's Madeline," Nora shouted.

The island grew in size as they approached. Adelle watched as the ferry glided smoothly toward the dock. It had been a short and uneventful ride, but she'd be glad to feel solid ground under her feet.

As they headed toward the Johnson's favorite picnic spot, Adelle felt herself relax. Among all the chatter she heard no one even mention Germany or the despised Huns—that's what some people called Germans. The war seemed very far away from this place. Maybe she could forget her worries about silly boys. But she could never forget about Karl. They still hadn't heard from him.

"So, what have you been up to this week?" Nora asked.

Adelle set her picnic basket down on a nearby log. "There's plenty to do, with Uncle Mike still not feeling like himself." She spread out a napkin and laid her sandwich on it. "I don't think he'd cleaned his house in years! Mother and I have been working like crazy putting it in order."

"I can imagine." Nora frowned at the contents of her basket. "Pickled herring yet again." She wrinkled up her nose.

"I have jam. Here, take half." Adelle handed Nora half her sandwich.

"Mmm, thanks." She took a bite. "Oooh, raspberry. Did you make it?"

"I helped Mother put it up last year. We did about a dozen jars." Adelle remembered the fun she and mother had canning the preserves. Both of them had been covered in sweet, red jam by the end of the day. It was before Karl had gone off. Happier times.

They ate their lunch in comfortable silence and when through, watched the younger children play with their jump ropes and kites. Jumping rope in the sand was tricky, so the little girls were trying to find grassy spots on the beach.

"Aren't you girls going to join the others?" Adelle's mother approached from where the adults were sitting.

"Oh, Mother, really, we're too old." Adelle tried to sound sophisticated.

Her mother simply laughed. "Of course, I should have

realized." She headed back over to where Nora's mother was sitting, still laughing gaily.

"I like your mom," Nora said.

"She's in a good mood today. She's usually pretty blue . . . at least lately." Adelle watched her mother, laughing and talking with Elizabeth Johnson. If only things could always be this way.

"Oh?"

"Ever since Karl went to war."

"Hmm. I know what you mean. My brother, Joey, is over there too. When we heard about Agnes' fiancé, we were all nearly crazy with worry. Mother was sure we'd be next to get a knock on the door."

"Do you worry about Joey a lot?"

"I think about him and Father, sure, but I'm not much of a worrier. Joey and Father will take good care of themselves. I'm sure of it."

"I wish I could be as sure about Karl." Adelle looked out over the lake. A few brave souls had gone in for a frigid swim.

"I saw Arthur once this week."

Adelle stiffened. "Oh?"

"He and some other boys were playing ball at the park. He talked to me for a long time after the game. I know you don't like him, but he's really not so bad. Howard is the one who talks him into pulling pranks."

"I can imagine." Adelle wondered what in the world Nora saw in that boy, but there was no point in commenting on it now. He wasn't anywhere around. Time to change the subject. "There weren't very many people on the ferry today."

"I suppose it's the war. Everyone cutting back on things—especially entertainments like this. Don't you just hate the Germans for getting us into this?" Nora blushed. "I'm sorry, I didn't mean . . ."

"It's all right. I'm American. And yes, I do hate the Germans for getting us into this stupid war." There, she'd actually said it out loud, in public. Adelle quickly looked over to where the adults were seated. Mother hadn't heard.

"I suppose that's how I would feel too. Of course you're American. I mean, you were born here, right?"

"Exactly. Just because my mother came over here from Germany means nothing to me. I'm here now and that's what counts." If that were true, why did she have this prickly, guilty feeling in her innards about how people were treating the German-Americans?

"Say, girls," Mrs. Johnson called to them. "Would you like to watch a ball game? There's one starting at the diamond."

"Want to?" Nora asked.

"Sure, we go to games all the time in Milwaukee. I like baseball."

"Hmm. I wonder if there'll be anyone interesting there," Nora said with a gleam in her eye.

That girl sure was boy crazy. But that was okay, as

long as Arthur wasn't around.

After trudging over the sand dunes and back to the baseball diamond, Adelle looked around the field at the players. "Do you know any of them?"

"I don't think so. Tourists come here from all over. I mostly only know Ashland people." Nora was quiet then, looking over the crowd for a familiar face. "Agnes' fiancé Mark used to play ball over here sometimes." Nora sighed.

Before he was killed in the war. Adelle remembered the angry look on Agnes' face at the ice cream social. "It must be terrible for your sister."

"That's why she didn't come today. She said she could not bear it."

Adelle shivered, thinking of Karl again. She glanced at the boy getting ready to bat. He looked about Karl's age, maybe a little younger. One day you're on a baseball field and the next, on a battle field.

"I hope we can come here again." Adelle squeezed Nora's hand. "It's nice here on the island."

"I hope so too." Nora smiled at her and Adelle felt like maybe they could be friends after all.

Sometime during the fifth inning, the sky grew cloudy and a threatening wind swept over the ball diamond. Elizabeth and Adelle's mother decided it would be best to go back on the early ferry before a storm blew up.

"Now we won't be able to build a bonfire on the beach tonight," Nora said as they hurried from the baseball field back to their picnic spot. Adelle and Nora quickly helped gather up the dishes and leftover food to save them from the encroaching waves.

"I'm afraid it won't be a good night for a fire. We'd start the whole woods ablaze." Nora's mother shook out the tablecloth.

As they boarded the ferry, Adelle realized they were too late to entirely avoid the bad weather. Although it wasn't raining yet, the wind had gotten even stronger and as the small craft took off from shore, it rocked from side to side in the choppy waves. Adelle shivered in her thin sweater, as she and Nora huddled on an end seat that was open to the winds.

Looking down into the violent gray waves, she shuddered, thinking of the *Lusitania*. That was the British ocean liner the Germans had sunk earlier in the war. Those poor people. Almost two thousand passengers. And more than a thousand had died, including many Americans on board. Drowning had to be the worst way to die.

Once again Adelle had the uneasy feeling that the lake was about to swallow her up. It was "her people" (that's what Mother called Germans) who had sunk the *Lusitania,* maybe even some of her own relatives who'd stayed behind in Germany when the rest of the family immigrated to the United States.

"Isn't this exciting?" Nora shouted over the wind and noise of the boat.

Adelle, surprised, looked over at her. Nora was actually enjoying the ride. "I guess so." She smiled weakly, wanting to be a good sport.

"I love it when the waves get choppy, it makes the ride that much more fun."

Nora didn't seem to worry about anything. Then Adelle looked over at her own mother and realized she was enjoying the ride as much as Nora. Uncle Mike said Mother loved Lake Superior, "so much like the sea." Most of the time, Mother was angry, but now she was clearly feeling . . . well, like a young girl. Adelle wondered if she'd ever figure her mother out.

Adelle looked toward shore, measuring in her mind how much farther they had to go. Through the spray she could just make out a group of people on the dock. "Look, tourists waiting for the ferry to take to Madeline Island. In this weather? They must be crazy."

"That is odd. Most people aren't like me." Nora laughed.

As they got off the ferry, however, Adelle realized these weren't all tourists. A number of men were circulating through the waiting crowd, handing out pieces of paper. Someone thrust one at her and the first thing she saw was:

HAMMER THE HUNS!!

in huge print at the top of the handbill.

Adelle quickly glanced over at her mother who'd just received a copy. *Oh, oh.* Quickly, Adelle went on to read the rest of it:

All patriotic citizens are urged to come to the meeting of the Council of Defense Thursday night at 7:00 PM at the Ashland Public Library. We will be discussing our latest relief project and Liberty Bond campaign. Your participation is crucial to defeating the Kaiser.

Adelle looked over at her mother again. She was no longer the laughing schoolgirl. She'd just finished reading the flyer and her face was flushed with anger. If only Uncle Mike were there. He could calm her down.

Before Adelle could say anything, her mother spoke in a tight but low voice to the man who had handed her the handbill. "I'll have you know that I'm a German-American and I resent being called a Hun. I have a son . . ."

She stopped abruptly.

Adelle could see she couldn't go on.

Mother crumpled up the flyer and threw it on the ground. The man who'd handed it to her looked stunned, but said nothing.

A Hun? Is that what people thought they were?

No, Adelle told herself, she didn't sink the *Lusitania*. The Germans weren't "her people." She was American. Not German-American, or a "hyphenate," as some people called them.

No matter how proud her mother might be of her German heritage, it meant nothing to Adelle.

She, too, crumpled up the copy of the flyer in her hand and let it float away. She would never again admit to anyone that German blood ran in her veins.

Chapter Five

The next morning, as soon as Adelle's chores were finished, she packed a picnic lunch and headed out to find Nora's house. Nora had invited Adelle over and suggested they take a picnic to the park.

"It's the big sandstone on Second Street, by St. Agnes' Church," Nora had said. Adelle found that it wasn't hard to spot—neither was the large gold knocker on the door.

The door opened. "I'm so glad you could come over," Nora gushed. "I'm anxious for you to meet some of my friends. They should be at the park today."

"That'll be great. I finished my chores early this morning so I could get here in time."

"Come on in."

Adelle stepped into the foyer and suddenly felt very small. Compared to Uncle Mike's house, Nora's was a mansion.

"I brought my lunch, like you suggested."

"Good. I made a quick lunch too and left a note for Mother. She's over at the church making bandages or something." Nora swept open the cupboards and started pulling supplies out. "Maybe someone interesting will be playing baseball." Nora giggled.

"I hadn't thought about that." Arthur would probably be there. *Well, too bad.* Adelle wasn't going to avoid a day of fun just because of some stupid boy.

"Can I see your room first?" Maybe she could put off the inevitable for just a little while.

"Sure. Follow me." Nora led her through the living room and up a staircase. At the landing they turned left and entered a bedroom. Agnes, Nora's sister, almost crashed into Adelle coming out of the room.

"Watch where you're going," Agnes snapped at her.

"I'm sorry."

"Oh, it's your little German friend." The older girl glared at Adelle.

Adelle's face went hot with anger. "I'm really not German. I was born here, in America."

Agnes turned on her heel and disappeared into another bedroom.

"Gosh, you shouldn't have said that." Nora whispered.

"Why not? It's true."

"I know, but, we try not to say anything to upset her since Mark's death."

Walking on eggshells. Just like we do around Mother since Karl left. You'd think he was dead, too. Adelle chased that thought away. "I think your sister really hates me."

"No. She's just grieving over Mark. I doubt she'll ever get over him."

Adelle wondered if that were true. *When you lost someone you loved with all your heart, did you ever forget them? Could you ever feel happy again?* She shook herself and concentrated on Nora's beautiful, but messy room. Clothes were on the floor. The bed was unmade. Mother would never allow Adelle to keep her room this messy.

"How do you like it?" Nora twirled around her room with arms outspread.

"I love it. It's so . . . comfortable."

"You mean messy." Nora laughed. "Ever since Father left, Mother has been less strict about these kinds of things. I think she actually enjoys not having to keep up with Father's high standards." Nora suddenly looked guilty. "I didn't mean to say we're glad Father's gone, I just meant . . ."

"It's all right. I know what you meant." But Adelle wondered. Maybe Nora's mother was distracted with worry too, just like Adelle's. Too distracted to care about things like tidying up. "The room's great. A little like mine at home."

"Do you miss Milwaukee terribly?"

Adelle looked around the room. "I am getting tired of Uncle Mike's snug little house. I love him dearly, but there's just nowhere for me to get away and be alone. I have to share a bedroom with my mother."

Nora flopped down on the bed "I can't imagine staying in Uncle Steven's old cabin."

Adelle joined her on the bed.

"What's your house in Milwaukee like?" Nora asked.

"It's a lot like yours. Maybe not quite as big, but lots bigger than the fish house!" Adelle fell dramatically backward onto the bed and laughed.

"I wish you could stay with us."

"Mother would never allow it. She needs my help."

Nora jumped off the bed in excitement. "Maybe you could persuade her to let you stay here just one night. Mayybeee . . . over the Fourth of July!"

Adelle sat up. "That would be fun. I'll work on it."

"Good. Let's go down to the kitchen. You can help me make some sandwiches."

"You're making more than one?" Adelle hopped off the bed and followed Nora downstairs and into the kitchen.

"Just in case anyone else there is hungry." Nora smiled as she took the bread from the bread box.

Nora had them make what seemed to Adelle enough sandwiches for the entire U.S. Army. Nora left a note for her mother and slipped her arm through Adelle's as they started out for the park.

Please, God, don't let Arthur and Howard be there, Adelle thought on the way to the park.

When they arrived, she noticed a large number of young people standing on the sidelines of a baseball game in progress. She glanced quickly from one person to the next, looking for the two boys.

"Do you see him?" Nora shaded her eyes against the

sun's glare as she looked over the crowd.

"Who?" Adelle played dumb.

"Arthur, of course," Nora whispered. "Ooh, there he is."

Oh well, Adelle thought, she knew her luck wouldn't hold forever.

"He's playing third base." Nora took Adelle's hand. "Let's find a place to sit."

Adelle was glad to see Arthur was busy playing ball. She squinted and studied each player. There was Howard, too, at shortstop.

They approached a group of girls about their own age. A tall girl with long blonde hair was waving frantically at Nora.

"Mary," Nora shouted and ran toward the girls. "I want you to meet my new friend, Adelle. Adelle, this is Mary. Adelle's from Milwaukee. She's spending the summer up here."

Mary glanced at Adelle and smiled. "Hi."

"So, who's winning?" Nora asked.

"Gee, I don't know, none of us are keeping score," Mary answered.

Nora turned to Adelle and whispered: "Sometimes she can be such a silly goose. I mean, if you want to talk to a boy about baseball, you'd better know who won at the end of the game." Nora pulled out a pencil and paper. "Do you know how to keep score?"

"I don't think so. I've never brought pencil and paper

to a game." Adelle laughed at Nora's intensity.

"My brother taught me everything I know about baseball. It doesn't hurt to have something in common with the boy you like."

"I suppose not." Adelle wondered again how Nora could go to so much trouble for a boy like Arthur.

As Nora combed the crowd, trying to find out the status of the game, Adelle studied some of the other people around her. Arthur and his friends were on the same team. The boy up at bat was slightly older and someone she didn't recognize. She wasn't as interested in boys as Nora seemed to be. Boys could be such foolish ninnies.

"There. I think I have it all figured out."

"What?"

"The game, silly. They're in the sixth inning and Arthur's team is behind, 8-4. It'll be a shame if they lose. He'll be in a sour mood."

It was clear Arthur meant a lot to Nora. Maybe he wasn't so bad. Maybe she should give him a chance.

All too soon the game was over. Arthur's team lost and he and his friends were heading their way—at least until Arthur saw Adelle. He hesitated. Good, she thought, he doesn't like being around me anymore than I like being around him. Nora, however, ran right over to him. Adelle followed, at a distance.

"I'm so sorry you lost, Arthur," Nora gushed. "Who was that nasty boy acting as umpire?"

"I don't know. Some kid from Washburn." Arthur

glanced around, avoiding Adelle's eyes.

Maybe it was time to forgive and forget. After all, Adelle needed some friends up here. She came forward and said, "Hello." She tried to smile confidently.

Nora swirled around. "You remember Adelle, Arthur." She turned back to him.

"Sure." Arthur studied his shoes.

"Are you hungry? I've brought sandwiches and lemonade for you and your friends," Nora asked.

"Ah, I don't know . . ." Arthur continued to look down, shuffling his feet.

"Sure, we'll take 'em. What've you got?" Howard peered over Arthur's shoulder as Nora opened her picnic basket.

"Lots of jam—no fish, Howard." Nora laughed. "Howie doesn't like fish, a cardinal sin when you live up here," she whispered to Adelle.

"Let's sit in the shade over there." Nora pointed to a large tree and the boys eagerly followed. Adelle wondered if Howard even recognized her. He wasn't acting all guilty like Arthur.

As soon as it was known that there was food to be had, Adelle and Nora were surrounded by boys. Adelle figured they were more interested in the food than the two of them and that was just fine with her. Besides, it was easy to ignore Arthur and Howard in this crowd.

"Hey, Howie, who do you think will win the World Series this year?" One of the boys asked.

"Oh, it's got to be the Yanks."

"Are you kidding? White Sox all the way."

"Hey, Arthur, you goin' down to Chicago for a game this summer? Like last year?"

"I dunno'. The train's more expensive this year."

"Take your car. You got one," Howie said.

"Nah. Pa says we can't 'cause of gas rationing." Arthur took a big bite of his sandwich.

"Yeah, well, we can thank the Krauts for that," Howie said and glanced at Adelle, but this time there was a twinkle in his eye.

So, he remembered her after all.

"Don't look at me." Adelle couldn't believe she'd said it. What could she possibly say next?

"You're a Kraut, right?"

"I am an American."

"Doubt it, with a name like Klein."

"So, what's your last name?" He wasn't going to get away with teasing this time.

"What's it to you?"

"Everybody in this country has relatives who came from somewhere else. What's the difference where they came from? I'm not German. I was born right here, in Milwaukee." Adelle's mother would not have agreed with that statement, but Adelle didn't care. She was tired of being German.

"Ooooh, Milwaukee." Howard made a high, spooky noise. "That city might as well be in Germany."

"So, what is your last name anyway?" Adelle wasn't giving up this fight.

"Billington, if you must know."

"What kind of a name is that?"

"Billington, I'll have you know, is a fine Yankee name. My ancestors came over on the first boat ever to America. You know, that boat with all those pilgrim people." Howard had a self-satisfied look on his face.

That boat? Didn't he even know the name of the Mayflower?

"What a dunce. Didn't you learn anything in history?" She was enjoying this.

"What do you mean?"

"The *Mayflower,* I believe is the ship, not a boat, you are referring to. Everyone knows the name of the *Mayflower.* At least if you'd paid attention in school."

The others were still chatting about baseball, so it was just Adelle and Howard engaged in this particular conversation. *Why was she wasting her time with him?*

She had to admit, though, there was something slightly likable about him, despite all his irritating qualities. Maybe it was that silly grin.

"Well, excuse me," Howard drew the word excuse out long and loud. "Little Miss Perfect."

Adelle let it go because she was curious about something. "If your ancestors were from out East, what brought your family to Ashland?"

Howard looked away, then down at the half-eaten

sandwich in his hand. "Um, well. My Pa, he wanted to be a fisherman."

"Oh, that's what my uncle does."

But instead of responding, Howard changed the subject once again. "Hey, do you wear those silly shorts with the suspenders I see in cartoons of Germans?"

"What? No, silly. Only boys wear those. They're called *Lederhosen*." Adelle thought quickly. "Nobody in my family would be caught dead in those things."

That was an outright lie. Her father and brother both belonged to a German singing group, and sometimes, such at Christmas, they would dress up in their traditional Bavarian outfits.

She had always wanted one of those beautiful Bavarian dresses the girls wore to the dances. A friend of hers had one. It was a lovely shade of dark green velvet, overlaid with a white apron. Decorative strings crisscrossed the bodice. The scalloped edges of the bottom of the apron stopped just short of the hem of the velvet *Dirndl* skirt.

Mother always said, "Some day." But some day never came around, and now with the war there wasn't any extra money for frivolous things like dresses. Besides, the dances had been banned. Too German.

What would Mother say if she could hear Adelle now, making fun of the things she loved? A pang of guilt prickled her, but she brushed it away.

"Yeah, those little shorts are really stupid looking,"

Howard commented and looked at her as if maybe he did not totally believe what she'd just said.

"You two still fighting about Germans over here?" Arthur interrupted.

"Yeah, let's not argue about this stupid stuff anymore, okay?" Nora agreed.

"We weren't arguing. Adelle agrees with me on every point. Don't you Adelle?"

Howard said it as if it were a challenge.

"Sure. I do." Her voice squeaked with the lie.

"Weren't we talking baseball?" Arthur spoke up. "Who cares about this dumb war anyway?"

A chorus of "I don'ts" rang out, and Adelle found her voice among them.

Chapter Six

Later, at her uncle's house, she tried to read more of *Twenty Thousand Leagues Under the Sea*. But the evil Captain Nemo and Professor Aronnax simply could not hold her interest. All the things she'd said that afternoon—especially agreeing that she didn't care about the war—was a lie. She tried to bat away her guilt like a pesky fly. But she should have told those boys about Karl. She should have stood up to their anti-German remarks. She should have been brave like her brother.

Maybe if she just talked sensibly to them they'd understand. Maybe even Howie. He didn't seem as bad today as when she first encountered him on the street.

A knock at the door interrupted her thoughts. "I'll get it," Mother called. "I wonder who that could be."

Adelle looked to the doorway, and standing in it was a short little man she didn't recognize.

"Good day, ma'am, and a lovely day it is. My name is Mr. Eric Lundstrom and I wonder if I could take a moment of your time?"

"That depends, Sir. Are you selling something?"

"Just the freedom of our great nation, ma'am."

Adelle watched as a crease formed on her mother's

forehead. She didn't care much for salesmen. "What exactly are you selling?" Her voice held more than a hint of annoyance.

"Why, Liberty Bonds, of course, ma'am."

The crease grew deeper. "Oh, I'm afraid we're not interested Mr. Lundstrom. We don't have a lot of extra money right now."

The man frowned and threw his shoulders back, standing up as tall as possible. "Why, ma'am, none of us has, but this is war. It's our duty to help our boys save the world from those bloodthirsty Huns."

Uh-oh, Adelle thought. He'd gone too far. Mother's face turned a deep crimson. *Please don't say anything stupid, Mother.*

Adelle's mother stood up tall and stepped forward to address the short little man, coming closer and closer with each word.

"Listen here, Mr. Lundstrom, we purchased bonds in Milwaukee. And I have a son fighting in this war. So I'd say our family has paid its dues doubly. Furthermore, my family came to this country from Germany to get away from the Kaiser, and I'll thank you not to refer to my ancestors or myself as a Hun, sir."

Mr. Lundstrom had been gradually backing up during Mother's outburst and now he almost fell backward as she slammed the door.

"Well, Emma, you certainly told him." Uncle Mike frowned and glanced at Adelle. "I just hope there aren't any repercussions," he said under his breath.

But Adelle had heard him. "What do you mean?"

He studied her for a long moment, as if trying to decide what to say. "I guess you're old enough, Addy."

"For what?" Now she really was curious.

"To be told the truth about people. Have you ever heard the word 'jingoism'?"

"Sure. Daddy uses it. He says it's patriotism gone overboard."

Uncle Mike sighed. "It's more than that, honey. Being in Milwaukee, you might not notice too much, but a lot of people around here don't take to German-Americans."

"Like Nora's friends."

He nodded. "Some people think all the Germans in these parts ought to be run out. Sent back to Germany, or at least Milwaukee. Now, your mother's made a pretty harsh statement to that gentleman. And I just hope that, well, it doesn't come back to haunt her."

Mother, who had been quietly, but furiously, cleaning off the table, finally spoke up. "The whole country's gone mad. I had to speak my mind, Mike."

He smiled. "You always did, Emma."

Even though Mike was smiling, there was concern in his eyes. Adelle chewed the inside of her lip. What if it got all over town that Mother refused to buy liberty bonds? They'd be in hot water for sure. She could just imagine what Arthur and his friends might say—or do.

"I've got a right to speak my mind."

"Father said a law was passed that says you don't," Adelle spoke up.

Mother looked at her in surprise. "I didn't say anything against the government of the United States. I just told the man not to call our people that despicable name. It's rude."

"Mother, they're not 'our people.'" Adelle surprised herself. Surely she'd be punished now.

But instead, her mother simply looked at her, disappointment written all over her face. She left the kitchen and retreated to the bedroom.

Mike looked at Adelle. "Uh-oh."

"I can't believe she didn't punish me. I shouldn't have said that."

"She's pretty upset." Uncle Mike took a sip of tea. "Her anger, it's really worry about Karl."

"Well, you'd never know it. She never mentions him."

"I thought I explained all that. And she did mention him—just now, to that man."

"I just don't understand her."

"I know, Addy, it's hard. Hard for you. Hard for your mother."

Adelle stood up, exasperated. "This war doesn't make any sense."

"Most wars don't."

"I just want to go back to Milwaukee. Won't you come with us?"

Uncle Mike's eyes grew sad again. "I may have to, eventually, but not yet, Addy, not yet."

Adelle went over and hugged him tight. Why was it so much easier to hug him than her mother? "I'm going to go outside and read for awhile, if that's all right. Is there anything I can get you first?"

"No, Addy girl, you just go ahead."

Adelle kissed his forehead and retrieved her book from the shelf. She took it outside and sprawled out in her uncle's old chaise lounge. Hopefully Captain Nemo could carry her away from the war and worries about Karl. Nemo and Aronnax were just putting on diving suits for a walk on the shallow floor of the sea.

One of the Nautilus's men presented me with a streamlined rifle whose butt was boilerplate steel, hollow inside, and of fairly large dimensions. This served as a tank for the compressed air. . . .

Above me I could see the calm surface of the ocean. We were walking on sand that was fine-grained and smooth, not wrinkled like beach sand. This dazzling carpet was a real mirror, throwing back the sun's rays with startling intensity. The outcome: an immense vista of reflections that penetrated every liquid molecule.

For a quarter of an hour, I trod this blazing sand,

strewn with tiny crumbs of seashell. Looming like a long reef, the *Nautilus*'s hull disappeared little by little.

We went ever onward, and these vast plains of sand seemed endless. My hands parted liquid curtains that closed again behind me, and my footprints faded swiftly under the water's pressure.

By then it was ten o'clock in the morning. The sun's rays hit the surface of the waves at a fairly oblique angle, as though passing through a prism; and when this light came in contact with flowers, rocks, buds, seashells, and polyps, the edges of these objects were shaded with all seven hues of the solar spectrum.

This riot of rainbow tints was a wonder, a feast for the eyes: a genuine kaleidoscope of red, green, yellow, orange, violet, indigo, and blue; in short, the whole palette of a color-happy painter!

She woke with a start. She'd been dreaming. German soldiers were firing at her and Karl, and to get away, the two of them had jumped into a deep pool of water. She was holding on to him for dear life, and trying to pull him forward, to run away, although they moved at a slow-motion crawl.

Adelle sat up and looked around, finally realizing

where she was—Uncle Mike's little cottage on Lake Superior.

Giving up on reading or sleep, she went into the house to prepare dinner.

Mother hardly spoke to anyone until the next day when it was time to get groceries at the store. As they approached the grocer's counter, Adelle noticed Howard's father glowering at them. She had a funny feeling another scene was about to erupt.

"Mother," Adelle touched her mother's arm lightly, "I think we should leave."

"What? It's almost our turn to order." Mother stepped up to the counter, behind a young woman with a baby in tow. When the grocer finished with them, he turned to Adelle's mother.

"Closed," he said as he put his sign on the counter.

Adelle felt as if a rock settled in her stomach. "Please, Mother, let's just go," she whispered.

At first, Mother looked confused. Then realization set in. "I beg your pardon, sir."

He pointed to the sign and said again, "Closed."

"But it's the middle of the day." Mother's voice rose, but Mr. Billington simply walked away.

Adelle's mother looked as if she wanted to say more, but instead glanced at Adelle. "You're right, *Liebchen.* I think it's time we left. We'll take our business else-where." Her words were spoken with no emotion, but Adelle could see the blush of anger on her face.

But Adelle was angry too. And it was time she let Mother know it.

"This is all your fault, Mother, for being so rude to that salesman yesterday. I'm sure it's all over town by now."

Adelle marched out of the store, not looking to see if Mother was behind her. She felt like a runaway train speeding down a hill, but she couldn't stop herself.

When Adelle knew her mother had caught up, words poured out. "You're so proud of your sacred German heritage. Well, guess what? No one else is. You're going to get us all thrown in jail, but you don't care. You had to go and defend the homeland, and with Karl in the middle of it all. Don't you even care what happens to him?"

Her mother looked at her, horrified, and in another second slapped Adelle hard, across her face.

Adelle felt the sting, but worse, she felt the weight of total rejection. Hot tears burned her eyes as she ran as fast as feet would take her all the way back to Uncle Mike's.

She couldn't believe what she'd just said to her mother. She never spoke to her that way, ever.

As she slowed her pace, guilt set in. Accusing her mother of not caring about Karl was wicked. Hadn't Uncle Mike explained her mother's odd behavior?

It was this wretched place: Ashland. That's what was making her so disrespectful. She hated Ashland almost as much as she hated being German.

She just had to convince Uncle Mike to go back to Milwaukee with them. Milwaukee: where life would be normal again.

Chapter Seven

The next three days Adelle buried herself in *Twenty Thousand Leagues Under the Sea*. Even the boring parts. At least she learned a lot about pearls and where they came from.

Mother was punishing her for her disrespectful outburst by confining her to the house. That was just fine with Adelle. She couldn't handle the questions she was sure to get if she chummed around with Nora and her friends right now anyway. She was sure everyone knew how the grocer had refused to serve them. Besides, Nora was in Bayfield, a town not far away up the shoreline, with her mother, spending a few days visiting and doing some errands.

As it turned out, there was only one grocer in town, so Nora's mother had gone shopping for them just before leaving. Even though Adelle felt bad about talking back, she was still angry that this situation was the fault of her mother and her principles.

Mother was now beginning to try to talk Uncle Mike into coming back to Milwaukee with them but he was being stubborn.

"You'll at least think about coming back with us at

the end of summer, Uncle Mike?" Adelle asked.

"I said I would think about it. That is all I can promise."

Mike and Adelle were sitting outdoors. Mother was inside, out of earshot.

"I'd really like to leave before the end of summer," Adelle confessed, as she chewed on her fingernails. "It's getting scary around here. And now the grocer won't let us shop."

"*Ach,* people have lost their senses. And your mother didn't help matters with the salesman."

"I just hope we don't get lynched before we decide to leave." Adelle shivered.

"Now, now, there's little chance of that."

Mother came out just then and began taking bedding off the wash line. *Why can't she just buy some more stupid Liberty Bonds and be done with it,* Adelle thought.

"Come help, Adelle."

Adelle got up reluctantly. When she took the first bed sheet off the line though, the aroma of freshly laundered linens took the edge off her anger. For a moment she buried her face in the clean, white cloth.

"The Johnsons will be back from Bayfield by the Fourth of July. Maybe we should go back to Milwaukee soon after they return. I'm afraid patriotism is going to reach a fever pitch around the Fourth. It would be best for us not to be here."

"See, Uncle, Mother thinks we could get lynched,

too."

"I never said that. But I doubt we'd be welcome at any of the festivities."

"Oh, Emma," Uncle Mike sighed. "It's not like you to run scared. I'm not ready to go to Milwaukee. I might never be. It's been a long time since I lived in a big city. Ashland suits me. I'll be fine here, when you go home." He was gazing out over the lake, a sad, far away look in his eyes.

"You can't stay here, Mike. You're not well enough to handle your fishing business all alone. And who will be your partner?"

"I'll manage."

Adelle saw her mother bite her lower lip as she bent over the wash basket, folding the last towel. Mother had once hoped that Karl might come up here and help Mike get back out fishing again, but Karl had other ideas. Now he was far away, in a foreign land, getting shot at if Adelle's nightmares were true. Adelle's chest filled with fear and for a moment she couldn't breathe. Why hadn't they heard from him?

"Ashland may suit you just fine, Mike, but we don't suit Ashland. I can't even go to the grocery store."

And whose fault is that? Adelle wanted to say, but couldn't. She was already under house arrest.

"But you love it up here, Emma, you always have."

"A person can't live on scenery. We'll come back. Some day, when all this is over." Mother sighed and picked up the basket.

Adelle felt a pang of sorrow and something else for her mother. Adelle understood what it was like to leave a place you loved. That's how she felt about Milwaukee. But there was something else different about her mother. It wasn't like her to give up and go home just because someone was disagreeable. Mother was a fighter, but it seemed like all the fight had left her.

Adelle wondered if it were her fault, for yelling at her so disrespectfully the other day.

"Yoo-hoo, hello everybody!"

Adelle looked up and there was Elizabeth Johnson, Nora's mother, walking up the path.

"Well, you got back sooner than I thought." Adelle's mother went over to her and put her basket back down.

"We just got in about an hour ago. I wanted to come right over and invite you to the July Fourth festivities."

A frown passed over Mother's face. "Oh, Elizabeth, I don't think that's a good idea. I doubt we'd be welcome."

"There's only a few simpleminded folks among us. You can go with my family. We'll all be together. It'll be fine."

"I was just telling Mike how I think we should go home before the Fourth. But he's being stubborn."

Elizabeth smiled. "As well he should. There's no reason for you to leave."

"Please, come in for tea. Adelle, would you put the kettle on?"

"Of course, Mother." Adelle went into the house, followed by the two women.

As Adelle filled the kettle with water, she wondered how she could talk Uncle Mike into leaving with them. It was pretty clear Mother wouldn't leave without him. Both of them were so stubborn.

"Adelle, I have news for you, too," Elizabeth began. "We would like to invite Adelle to spend the night with us on the Fourth, if that's all right with you, Emma."

Mother frowned. "Hmm. I'm not sure I should let such a disrespectful child have a night of freedom."

"Oh, I'm sorry, I didn't realize Adelle was being punished." Elizabeth sat down on the couch.

"Let the child go, Emma." The door slammed as Uncle Mike followed them into the house. "I think she paid for her crime these last few days, holed up in this old shack." He winked at Adelle.

"The time she's been 'holed up,' as you say, should not count because her friend was away anyway. So by rights, she should be punished now that Nora is home."

If she couldn't go home, it would be nice to at least have one night of fun. Adelle was about to protest when Mike signaled her with a quick motion of his hand behind his back to keep still.

"Now, Emma. You can't blame the child for having spunk. She comes by it naturally." He smiled mischievously at Mother.

"You're incorrigible." But there was a twinkle in

Mother's eye. Adelle thought the brother and sister must love each other very much. Like she and Karl. Adelle's chest tightened again. *No, she would try not to worry all the time about him.*

Then, it occurred to Adelle. Is that what her mother had been doing all these months? Forcing herself not to think about Karl? Is that why she rarely talked about him? What if Mother were having nightmares, too?

Her mother sighed. "I'll think about letting her go to Nora's for a night—if she stays on her best behavior until then."

She turned to Adelle. "No more talking back. And put these things away." Mother handed her the basket full of clean bedding.

"Oh, no, Mother. I wouldn't. Talk back, I mean." She took the basket and hurried to the bedroom.

At least now she had something to look forward to before they left this God-forsaken place. Adelle looked over her shoulder, as if Mother could read her thoughts.

Hooray! Adelle would get to stay at Nora's overnight. Maybe they could get away with staying up all night chatting if they were really quiet. To her surprise, she even found herself wondering if Howard would be at the picnic. If nothing else, the Fourth of July would surely be the most exciting night since she arrived in Ashland.

Chapter Eight

Finally, the Fourth of July arrived. When Adelle woke up to see rain and fog out her window, she rubbed her eyes and pulled the covers over her head.

"Time's a wastin', Addy. Up and at 'em!" Uncle Mike called from the kitchen a few minutes later.

"Hmmm," she mumbled through the sheets. "Why should I get up? It's raining. The picnic will be cancelled."

"What's that, Addy? Can't hear you."

She rolled out of bed. She might as well get up. If she went back to sleep she'd just have another bad dream about Karl. Adelle grabbed her bathrobe, and slipped into her house slippers. It was always cold in Uncle Mike's house in the morning. Even in July.

She padded out to the kitchen while tying her robe tight around her. "I said, it's raining. The picnic will be cancelled."

"Oh, it'll clear up by noon. I know the weather in these parts. It's just a low-hanging fog. No real storms coming."

She rubbed her eyes and squinted out the window. "It's low-hanging all right. Right down to the ground."

Adelle laughed and looked around the small house. "Where's Mother?"

"Over at Elizabeth's, cooking for the big day. There's more room in that kitchen. I get to cook breakfast for you." Uncle Mike pulled out a chair for her.

The wrinkles around his eyes formed into a smile as Adelle sat down. He seemed to have a lot of energy today. Surely he was well enough to travel. But she didn't want to bring up the subject of him moving to Milwaukee and see his eyes turn all sad again.

"Maybe I should go over to Nora's too," suggested Adelle, "when I'm finished with chores here. They could probably use my help."

"Good idea. I'll meet all of you over at the park later."

"Are you sure you'll be okay here, Uncle Mike? You could go with me to the Johnsons." She hadn't heard him cough in awhile, but still . . .

"Oh, I'll be just fine, child. I've got to be on my own sooner or later."

He's really thinking of staying here by himself. Mother has just got to talk him out of that.

When she got to Nora's the rain had already stopped, even though the fog was still so thick Adelle almost missed Nora's house. Agnes answered her knock.

"Come in." This time the older girl didn't glare at Adelle anyway. "Nora's in the kitchen."

Just then there was the sound of a dish crashing to the floor.

Adelle headed for the kitchen, and there was Nora kneeling on the floor. "Look what I did. Broke the butter dish. At least it's not our best."

Adelle knelt down, careful to avoid the crushed shards, and began to help. "Where's our mothers? I thought they'd be here cooking."

"All finished. They went over to the park already. I'm just making sandwiches for us."

Adelle spotted four sandwiches on the counter. "You planning on eating a lot?"

"Some friends are meeting us at the park." Nora's eyes twinkled with mischief.

"Arthur and Howard?"

"Uh-huh," Nora answered.

Adelle didn't know how to feel about this news. The boys were kind of a pain and she hadn't totally forgiven them for teasing her. Also, their presence made her act in a way that she didn't really like—going along with their criticism of German people.

On the other hand, Howard had been a little nicer to her the last time she saw him. Maybe this time she'd have the nerve to tell him how she really felt about this war. After all, he didn't even know she had a brother in it.

Nora swept up the remainder of the broken dish as Adelle held the dustpan. After everything was cleaned up, Nora brushed herself off. "Let me take your overnight bag upstairs."

Nora took the bag from Adelle. "Hope you brought your swim suit."

"Swim suit?" Adelle hadn't considered swimming the frigid waters of Lake Superior.

"Never mind. I'll lend you one of mine."

"We're going swimming?"

"We always do on the Fourth. But, don't tell anyone," Nora's voice grew conspiratorial. "This year we're going to a place where the older kids swim. I'm not telling my mother."

Nora looked at the ceiling as if trying to figure something out. "In fact, we better put our bathing suits on here, under our clothes. I don't want Mother to know where we're going."

Adelle was leery of this plan. What had she told Uncle Mike about how she felt about Lake Superior? Too big and black and foreboding. So different from Lake Michigan. "Is it safe?"

"Safe?" Nora repeated the word, like it was the silliest thing she'd ever heard. "Of course it's safe."

"Well, then, why can't you tell your mother?"

"Oh, she worries about everything since Father and Joey went off to war. Things she didn't used to worry about. And there's another reason." Nora giggled.

Adelle just looked at her questioningly.

"The older kids. The ones who are going steady. They

go out there. Mother thinks they're a bad influence on me." She laughed again and packed up the sandwiches.

Adelle was getting a pretty good idea of what Nora's mother meant. There were similar places in Milwaukee on Lake Michigan where teenagers hung out and didn't always behave properly.

"Let's go up to my room and change," Nora said as she led Adelle out of the kitchen.

After changing, they came back down the stairs. "Ready to go?" Nora asked.

"Ready as I'll ever be."

"Oh, don't worry. It'll be fine."

But Adelle wasn't so sure. All the way to the park she thought about how she should talk to Howard today. She'd be brave and tell him exactly what she thought. And that place they were going to swim. It didn't sound like a good idea to her.

Then, she scolded herself. *Don't be such a coward. Take a risk. Have some fun.* She said it over and over in her mind until they got to the park. Nora, chatting all the way, had no idea.

When they arrived at the park, it was still damp. But the fog had mostly lifted, and patches of blue could be seen scattered among the light, low-floating clouds. Their mothers were the only ones there.

"Hello, girls," Elizabeth called to them.

"Hello, Mrs. Johnson," Adelle called back.

"Mother, we're going to take a walk." Nora stated it as

a fact, rather than a request.

"All right, but be careful. Don't go too far."

"We'll be careful, Mother," Nora answered and took Adelle by the arm, whispering: "We're going to have an adventure."

Adelle felt positively wicked, but in a fun way. As they got out of earshot of their mothers, she asked: "Where exactly are we going?"

"About a mile down the beach."

"That sounds good." Adelle still wasn't sure, but when in Rome, do as the Romans do, her father always said.

Nora led Adelle along the main path until it disappeared. Then she broke off onto more rugged terrain up and down rocky bluffs.

Adelle was soon out of breath. "Where in the world are we going?"

"You'll see," Nora said mysteriously.

Finally, Adelle spotted what must be their destination. At the bottom of one of the rocky bluffs lay a clean white beach, deserted except for a few gulls combing the sand for lunch. The lake was calm, the sand undisturbed except for the birds' scratchy claw prints.

"Oh, my goodness. This is a beautiful place. Do you come here often?" Adelle grabbed onto stubby bushes as she slid carefully down the bluff. There was no real path.

"No. But Agnes did, with her fiancé. I followed them once, just to see where they were going." There was a sad, thoughtful tone to Nora's voice.

Finally down the hill, Nora picked a flat spot to sit. She worked her feet into the warm sand and looked out at the lake waters. "Now, all we have to do is wait."

"What are we waiting for?" Adelle collapsed into the sand beside her.

"The boys, silly." Nora pulled out the sandwiches from under her blouse.

Adelle hadn't noticed her hide them. "Oh."

Boys or no boys, Adelle was broiling with all the layers of clothing she had on. Rivulets of sweat ran down inside her blouse. In the protected cove, the sand was hotter than she expected, even with that morning's rain, and the sun was blazing now. Uncle Mike was right about the weather.

Adelle looked at the clear, cool water. To her own surprise, she said, "You want to go in?"

"You read my mind. Race you." Nora stripped off her outer clothes and ran into the water up to her knees. Then stopped short. "*Brrrr.*"

Adelle followed and when the icy water met her burning feet, it felt like heaven. But when the water got up to her knees, she looked at Nora. "Double-*brrr.*"

"Let's just dive in, real quick. It's the best way," Nora said.

Adelle knew that was true. Back in Milwaukee, Lake Michigan was plenty cold itself, although not quite as chilly as the waters of Superior. Summoning all her courage, she faced the lake. *It was now or never.* Adelle ran as far as she could deeper into the water and then dove in.

Nora followed and came up screaming, "Wow, that's cold!"

After a while, the girls became more accustomed to the cool waters. Adelle floated on her back for awhile, letting the gentle waves lift her ever so carefully. The lake still made her a little nervous, but today it reminded her of Lake Michigan and all the summers she'd spent swimming with her friends. If only she could stay on these waves forever. She wouldn't have to worry about Karl, or the war, or what other people thought of her.

"Hey, Arthur!" Nora suddenly called out.

Adelle's peaceful mood shattered. Sure, she knew they were coming. But still, it could have been more fun if it were just she and Nora. She swam into the shallows and stood up, the cool breeze prickling her like tiny icicles.

Arthur and Howard, already dressed in bathing suits, were approaching from the woods. The girls ran up onto the beach, shivering.

"How's the water?" Howard asked Adelle.

Nora answered before Adelle had a chance to open her mouth. "Oh, it's really warm. You'll see." She winked at Adelle.

"Yeah, I'll bet," Arthur answered, but dashed toward the lake anyway. Howard looked skeptical.

"Well?" Nora prodded.

"I think I'll wait." Howard looked out at the water.

Just then, Arthur let out a piercing howl as he plunged into the lake.

Nora and Howard laughed. Adelle joined in. *Serves him right,* she thought.

"We'd better go swimming now," suggested Nora. "If we're gone too long, our mothers will get nervous. And we've got to dry off before we get back." Nora headed toward the water. Adelle followed, but when she got back in, she paddled in the other direction, away from Arthur and Nora's noisy horseplay.

"Yow!" Howard shouted as he finally joined them.

"C'mon over, Adelle, let's play chicken," Nora yelled.

"Sure," Arthur and Howard agreed in unison.

Adelle had played it a thousand times at home with friends. But she didn't really know these boys very well and worse, she didn't trust them. "I don't know . . ."

"C'mon, Adelle, don't be a spoil-sport. It'll only work if you play. No one else is here."

Where were all the teenagers that Nora said came here? Adelle guessed it was too early in the day for them. "Okay. I'm coming." She swam over.

Arthur ducked under the water while Nora climbed up on his shoulders. Adelle followed suit with Howard. How did she get herself into this?

The first time she fell off Howard's shoulders, she was a little stunned by the cold, deep water, but the next time she was ready for Nora. Finally, she managed to knock Nora off of Arthur. "Gotcha'!"

As Nora went under, Arthur teased her by holding her under for a few seconds. Nora came up sputtering. "Arthur, I'll get you for that!" But she was laughing and back up on Arthur's shoulders in a minute.

Nora pushed hard on Adelle's palms as they both fought to get the other one down. Suddenly Adelle lost her balance and found herself swimming upside down. She opened her eyes and focused on the bottom, but when she tried to stand up she found the water too deep. She swam to the shallows.

When she got there, though, Howard was waiting for her. He pulled her hair and pushed her under. Kicking furiously, she struggled against him, but he grabbed both her legs and she went deeper.

She didn't know at first if she was more angry or scared. Friends had dunked her in Lake Michigan plenty of times, but was Howard being mean on purpose? Because she was a 'Kraut?' If only she could get hold of some part of him—scratch him with her fingernails, anything to stop him. But he was too tall and strong for her.

Now he had his hands on her head again, pushing her farther and farther down. It was getting harder to hold her breath. Why was he being so mean? Her chest was about to explode and for the first time she felt real panic. Like Professor Aronnax, she was a prisoner of the deep.

Then all her anger, all her fear, transformed itself into a fearsome energy. She kicked Howard's knees as hard as possible. He fell backwards, releasing her.

Adelle surfaced, coughing and choking. She looked around, spotted the shore, and headed toward it, but not before she turned to Howard.

"You jerk, you almost drowned me."

She stomped to shore and pulled her clothes over her wet suit.

"Hey," Howard called. "I was just joking."

"Yeah, some joke," she said to herself. And to think she thought they were actually getting along the other day. He was just like all the other people in this stupid town. He hated her because she was German.

She was freezing, but she'd have to dry off first before heading back. She didn't want Mother to know she'd gone swimming in such an out-of-the-way place. Nora joined her soon on the beach.

"Sorry about that, Adelle. Howie can go overboard sometimes. I guess he's just like his father."

Howard walked up just then. "Geez, Nora, is that what you think?"

He looked upset, but Adelle couldn't tell if he was mad or just sad about something. Howard walked away, pulled his clothes on over his bathing suit and started to climb the bluff.

"Howie, where you goin'?" Arthur hollered.

Howard didn't answer.

The festive mood was shattered. Even the sun had gone behind gray clouds.

"I guess we better dry off and go back to the park." Nora sounded disappointed.

"Yeah, I'll go catch up with Howie. See what he's mad about now." Arthur pulled his clothes on quickly and left.

"I don't know what gets into Howard sometimes." Nora sighed.

"He really scared me. I thought I was going to drown." Adelle watched as Arthur caught up with Howard high above them on the bluff.

"Sometimes he can be so nice, and other times – well, you were right. He can be a real jerk."

"I suppose it's 'cause I'm German." Adelle felt the sun come out from behind the clouds again. It felt warm and comforting after her cold brush with disaster.

"I don't know. Maybe. But he can be a jerk to anyone, anytime. He's moody. It's weird."

"What did you mean about his father?" Adelle remembered Uncle Mike referring to Howard's father once with distaste.

"Oh, everybody knows. His father is an old 'souse' and a much bigger jerk than Howie."

"You mean he drinks too much?"

"Uh-huh. Way too much." Nora stretched. "Shall we

go? I think we'll be plenty dried off after climbing that bluff."

"Yeah, I think so too."

When they arrived back at the picnic grounds, it seemed the whole town was there. Wicker baskets were open everywhere, and throngs of people were busy setting their tables.

"Where were you girls?" Nora's mother, Elizabeth, looked them over, frowning.

Can she tell that the clothes we put on over our swim suits are still a little damp? wondered Adelle.

"Nowhere." Nora grabbed a handful of strawberries from the bowl on the picnic table. She sat down next to her mother.

"You weren't on that beach where all the young people congregate, were you young lady?"

"Um . . ." Nora answered.

"Nora—how many times have I told you not go there?"

"Now, now," Uncle Mike interrupted. "The children need to be able to explore. I'm sure you did a little of that at their age." He winked and glanced from Elizabeth to Adelle.

"They could have drowned, Mike." Adelle's mother set out a large bowl of potato salad.

Adelle poured herself a glass of lemonade.

Uncle Mike glanced at her. "But you see, Emma, they

99

didn't drown. Have a good time, Addy?"

"Just peachy." Adelle looked at Uncle Mike with meaning.

Uncle Mike looked from Adelle to her mother, who hadn't noticed Adelle's annoyed tone of voice.

"Help me set the table, Nora. I'm sure everyone is starved by now." Elizabeth Johnson handed Nora a tall stack of china dishes. "Now be careful, Nora, they may be our everyday dishes, but we can't afford new ones right now."

The day dragged on. Adelle and Nora played checkers. What had been a much-anticipated outing had turned into a complete disaster. *All because of those boys. Why was Nora so set on spending every moment with Arthur?*

Adelle had to admit that the other day, when she and Howard talked, he had been pretty nice. But after today she didn't care if she ever saw him again.

Finally, it was time for the fireworks to start. A man's voice, amplified by a megaphone, boomed out over the park: "Attention, ladies and gentlemen."

Adelle looked toward the speaker. In the twilight, she could just see three men on a platform. One was the speaker. The other two had a huge American flag, with one man on each side of it, holding it up with tall wooden dowels that were attached to each end.

"We would like to dedicate this evening's fireworks display to our brave young men overseas."

A lead ball of guilt settled into Adelle's stomach. She had been so wrapped up in her own little troubles with Howard, she hadn't thought of Karl all day. Would they ever hear from him?

"To all the fine young men . . ." A man in the audience stood up. Then, someone else stood. Next, someone started singing the "Star Spangled Banner."

Soon, everyone joined in.

Adelle didn't know all the words, but she sang as best she could with a lump in her throat. *Please, God,* she prayed. *Please keep Karl safe.*

Adelle looked over at her mother. She was singing, too—but were those tears in her eyes?

When the song was over, a wave of applause surged through the crowd. Then, a low mumbling started, and as it grew louder, Adelle understood what people were saying.

"Hammer the Hun, kill the Kaiser," the crowd chanted. "Death to all Krauts."

Anger burned red hot through Adelle. *My brother is in the war—and he's German,* she wanted to shout.

Suddenly, she felt her mother's arm around her.

"It's time we were going, Adelle." Mother took her daughter's hand firmly in her own.

"What about the overnight at Nora's?" *It could still be fun, couldn't it?*

"Just come along," was all Mother replied.

Uncle Mike got up quietly and joined them. Mother

whispered something to Elizabeth—probably canceling the overnight, Adelle thought—and then maneuvered both Adelle and Mike through the crowd.

As they made their way, Adelle thought she heard whisperings and felt as if the whole crowd were watching her. Her heart nearly beat out of her chest. What more could happen this day?

The walk back to Uncle Mike's seemed longer than usual. Adelle heard the fireworks going off overhead, but she didn't even look up to see them. Once home, she put water on for tea. Mother didn't have to ask.

"Mike, I wish you would give some thought to going back to Milwaukee with us." Her mother was starting in on Mike again.

"Oh, Emma." Mike sighed. He didn't seem to have the energy to argue with her tonight. Maybe he would change his mind after all.

The kettle began to whistle, and Adelle jumped up to serve the tea. She was too anxious to even think about going to bed. The adults sipped their tea without speaking, and the silence was making Adelle fidgety. She felt as if she might jump right out of her skin.

It grew later, and the tea was cold, but the grown-ups weren't making a move toward bed, so Adelle didn't either. The ticking of the clock was the only sound. No one seemed to have a thing to say. The quiet was making her crazy, but she knew that if she tried reading her book she'd never be able to concentrate. It seemed like the night was waiting—waiting for something to happen.

Boom! All three of them jumped. Adelle ran to the window. "What was that?"

"Just a firecracker." Uncle Mike joined her at the window.

"That was a pretty loud one." Adelle's mother came over to look, but there was nothing to see.

Adelle squinted into the darkness. "Do you hear something else?" she asked.

"No," Mother and Uncle Mike replied together.

But Adelle was sure she heard something. It was like a rumbling sound, or . . .

She ran to the door and went out into Mike's front yard.

"Adelaide, where do you think you're going?" Her mother was right behind her.

It was the same noise she heard at the park. A low mumbling. Adelle cupped her hands behind her ears so she could better hear. "Don't you hear it?" She looked up at her mother.

Mother's face was a blank, but Adelle was sure she could hear it too now. Uncle Mike joined them in the yard and he put his hand on Adelle's shoulder. "We should go in."

"No. I want to see what's going on."

"It's not safe, Addy."

The sound grew nearer, and now she could make

out the words of the chant: "Hammer the Hun, kill the Kaiser, death to all Krauts."

They were coming around the corner. In the darkness, Adelle couldn't make out who was in the group, but it wasn't all that large—maybe ten people or so.

'We'd better get back into the house." Her mother put her hands on Adelle's shoulders and tried to steer her towards the house.

But Adelle didn't move. Who were these people who shouted into the night? Part of her wanted to run away and hide, but another voice inside told her she must be brave for once. Brave for Karl.

"There's one, let's get him!" Someone from the crowd shouted, and before she knew what was happening, the group swarmed into Uncle Mike's front yard.

"Get the child in the house, Emma," Mike said as he walked toward the revelers.

Mother's fingernails were digging into Adelle's shoulders, but Adelle wriggled away and ran after her uncle.

"Adelle, I demand you get into the house," her mother shouted.

"That's right, little girl. You don't want to see your uncle here, tarred and feathered, do you?" a slurred voice cried out.

Howard's father. Of course, he would be the instigator. Then Adelle noticed two large, burly men restraining a tall, thin man with a beard, struggling a little but unable to break free. Clearly the tall man did not want to be there.

Were they going to tar and feather him?

Well, they weren't going to do it to her uncle. She wouldn't let them. Adelle dashed out ahead of Uncle Mike. She wasn't sure what she was going to do, but the anger that had been building up in her since earlier in the day when Howard had dunked her boiled over.

"You're not going to hurt my uncle."

"Little girl, do as your Kraut mother says, and go back into the house," Howard's father, Mr. Billington, seemed barely able to stand. Of course, the lot of them were probably drunk.

"No, I won't," she shouted back at him. "Get out of our yard!"

"Adelle," her uncle said sharply and Adelle looked at him, surprised. He never called her anything but Addy. "You listen to your mother."

"I'm sorry, Uncle Mike, but I can't."

She turned back to the crowd. "You're not taking my uncle anywhere."

People in the group began whispering, mumbling. Most of them had that glazed look in their eyes that meant they'd drunk too much. Adelle smelled liquor in the air. The humid night made the air stale, like a simmering stew of bad smells.

She glanced at the thin man with the scholarly beard that several of them were holding. The man's eye had swelled up from a recent blow. Blood trickled out of the corner of his mouth.

Adelle's rage grew like a fire in her chest.

"So, this is your idea of fun? Getting drunk and beating up on people? Aren't you all a little bit too old to be pulling pranks?"

Howard's father took a wobbly but threatening step toward Uncle Mike. Adelle made a move to stand between the two of them, facing the drunk grocer. She felt like she was watching a different girl, not herself. It was as if someone else had inhabited her body. Someone with courage.

Uncle Mike grabbed her from behind. She tried to break free, but he held firm.

"Aw, come on," someone in the crowd muttered, slurring his words. "Just leave the old man alone. We don't want to get involved with some kid. We've got bigger fish to fry." One of the large men pointed to the tall, thin man he had collared.

Howard's father spit at Adelle and Uncle Mike, but missed. His stale breath, reeking of alcohol and tobacco, almost knocked Adelle over. He looked around and realized the others in the crowd were starting to back away. Uncertain, Mr. Billington wavered. Then, he turned on his heel and left, following the mob that was still muttering things about Huns and Krauts. A few seconds passed, and then they were gone. All that was left was a faint scent of putrid air.

Then even that was cleared away by a light breeze off the lake, accompanied by the distant sound of small waves against the invisible shore.

Adelle turned to her uncle and took his hand. She was shaking, and Uncle Mike put his arm around her to steady her.

"You did a brave thing, Addy. Maybe not so smart, but brave for sure."

Her mother was still outside, waiting for them at the door. Adelle expected to be scolded, but her mother just looked at her, tears in her eyes.

"I think she's a chip off the old block, Emma," Mike said as they entered the house.

Her mother just nodded and squeezed Adelle's shoulder.

Adelle felt like she had just hiked up a Lake Superior bluff. She was exhausted, but the anger was gone.

Chapter Nine

Later that evening, a sudden squall blew in off the lake, beating on the roof in rolling bursts of wind and rain.

It kept all three inhabitants of Uncle Mike's house awake for a long time, each in their bed, until the storm passed and the deep silence of the night returned.

The next morning, the sun was out again, and the thin grasses and small bushes surrounding the little cottage glistened in the sunlight. After breakfast, Uncle Mike went into town with Mother to visit Elizabeth Johnson. They insisted Adelle stay home, safely inside the cottage, until they found out what had happened with the gang the previous night.

So Adelle was just reading the final pages of *Twenty Thousand Leagues Under the Sea* when she heard the postman come. Aching for something to do, she went outside to meet him.

"How 'bout that." He squinted into the early morning light. "Two in one week. Must be something special." He glanced at Adelle and back at the letter.

It was from Father. Adelle's heart seemed to stop. Father had been methodical, writing just once a week.

They'd already heard from him this week, so what could this be?

It was an especially fat letter. She turned it over in her hand. It was addressed to both her and her mother. Could she open it? Would Mother be angry if she didn't wait?

Was it news about Karl? Surely if something dreadful had happened, Father would have taken the train up, not simply written a letter.

Adelle put the letter on the table. She would wait for Mother.

She picked up her book, but couldn't concentrate. The *Nautilus* was being pulled into a dangerous whirlpool that threatened the survival of the craft and crew. But her body wouldn't keep still enough to read.

She set down the book and got up and paced. What could she do? Keep busy. Clean. So Adelle spent the next hour racing throughout the little house, dusting every corner and scrubbing every spot and stain she could find.

Finally, she heard voices coming up the walk.

"Mother, mother, we got a letter from Father," Adelle shouted as she ran out the door.

A look of alarm passed over her mother's face. Elizabeth Johnson was with her, as was Nora and Uncle Mike.

Nora's mother was reassuring. "Now, Emma, wait and see. It could be good news." Mrs. Johnson patted

Emma on the shoulder, but her eyes held concern.

"But we just heard from him a day or two ago. He only writes once a week and . . ."

Adelle looked at Uncle Mike, hoping for reassurance. He said nothing, just shook his head slightly, which meant, *keep still*.

Everyone gathered in the kitchen. Nora waved and pointed to something in her hand, but Adelle was too occupied with Father's letter to wonder what it was.

"Girls, put on some tea," Nora's mother looked pointedly at Nora and Adelle.

Grown-ups. They always want to keep the children busy when there's a crisis. Adelle prayed this wasn't one of those times.

She went to put water on the stove, and Nora followed.

"I have something for you," her friend whispered.

"My overnight bag?" Adelle had noticed Nora carrying it in, and remembered that Mother had steered them home so quickly the night before after the fireworks in the park that she hadn't been able to go to Nora's to pick it up.

But instead, Nora handed Adelle a crumpled piece of paper.

"What's this?" Adelle wasn't interested. Instead, she looked over at her mother, sitting at the table now, holding Father's letter in her hand, and not opening it. "Why doesn't she open it?" Adelle whispered, as the adults were silent, looking expectantly at Mother.

"Adelle, she will," Nora said. "It won't be bad." She squeezed Adelle's hand with the paper in it. "Read it."

But she couldn't. Whatever was in her hand couldn't be about Karl, and that's all she cared about right now. She stuffed the bit of paper in her apron pocket.

"Here," she said, as she handed Nora the teapot. "The tea is over there in that canister. The cozy is in one of the drawers." Adelle thought she would burst, waiting for her mother to open the letter. She was just about to say so when a glance from Uncle Mike silenced her. *Oh, dear God,* she prayed, *don't let it be bad news.*

"Go ahead, Emma, it'll be all right." Mrs. Johnson patted Mother's hand.

Adelle's mother turned the letter over and, sliding one finger slowly under the closure, handled the letter cautiously, as if it were a hot iron about to burn her.

Adelle held her breath and watched, her heart beating wildly. Mother took the sheets of stationary out of the envelope, one of which looked like the paper Father used. The others were different, crinkled and a grayish color. Mother's eyes seemed to race over the first sheet, then, she dropped all of them and burst into tears.

"No," Adelle shouted and ran to scoop them up. "He can't be . . ."

"Oh, Addy, I'm sorry, no, no, Karl is all right." Mother was weeping so hard she barely got the words out. "Finally a letter from him."

Mother hadn't called her Addy since Karl left. Surely something was wrong. Adelle sat on the floor and gathered the papers together. The first sheet was as she suspected: a short note from her father, explaining that he'd received this letter from Karl and wanted to send it along. Then Adelle picked up the rest of the sheets.

"Read it, Addy, please. I can't just now." Her mother smiled at her through tears.

The pages were neatly numbered in Karl's handwriting. Adelle put them in order, hands shaking with excitement.

"Dear Mom, Pop and my spoiled Kid Sister," Adelle began. She looked up. "I'll get him for that," she said, her voice close to breaking.

She continued.

"I don't know how much news you get in the States, but the 32nd Division took heavy fire since May. I hardly have a moment to myself to eat or wash, much less get out a letter. Where I am right now, well, I can't say. First, let me tell you what we did when we first arrived in France.

"Before we got sent to the front, we got to go to the beach every day. The water was freezing—even colder than Lake Michigan—but it was refreshing and kept us clean. I know how much you like the Lake in summer, Sis. You would have loved the ocean. The chaplain had a tent set up with a piano in it. Can you imagine that? I don't know where he got it from, but in the evenings he played and a couple of us would stand around and sing."

Adelle stopped reading, picturing Karl standing around the piano, singing with his friends, just like he did at home. The lump in her throat grew larger. She took a deep breath and went on.

"Now for the best news. I'm coming home."

Adelle stopped and just stared at the page. Her mother let out a cry and everyone else said, "Thank God."

But Adelle saw the next words. How would she be able to say them? *Be brave,* she told herself, *just like last night.*

"Yes, I'm coming home. See, I got this little injury. Well, not so little I guess. At first they thought they'd have to take my leg off."

Adelle's mother cried out, "Oh, my sweet boy."

"Now, Emma, he sounds fine, doesn't he?" Uncle Mike went over and put his arm around her. "Go on, Addy, finish up."

"But they got the infection under control. Still, my leg's pretty mangled. I won't be of much use to them over here anymore so they're shipping me back to the States. In fact, by the time you get this I'll be on my way home. Not sure I'll be dancing for awhile. But Sis, I expect to see you dancing when this war is over. I'll be seeing you all soon. Love, Karl.

"Oh, P.S. Ask Uncle Mike if he could use a slightly lame fishing partner."

Adelle concentrated on slowly folding the papers neatly. She was still fighting tears, both of joy and worry. *Just how bad was his injury?* she wondered. He mentioned how he couldn't dance for awhile. Maybe never? But he was alive and that's what counted. Alive and coming home.

"Well, how about that?" Uncle Mike had a big smile. "Now, Emma, will you stop trying to convince me to go back to Milwaukee with you? The boy wants to come up here." Uncle Mike's face was glowing.

It was the happiest Adelle had seen him since they arrived. She got up and handed the letter to Mother. Mother took the letter, then reached out to Adelle, sobbing. "Our sweet boy is coming home."

Adelle finally let go too, letting all the tears flow. All the time Karl was away at war and Mother never mentioning him, all the anger Adelle felt because of her silence, it all melted away. Uncle Mike was right. Mother had been too afraid, too scared to talk about Karl.

"This is a day for celebrating," Mrs. Johnson said. The tea kettle began to howl just then, so Adelle quickly went to it.

Nora followed her and whispered again, "Open the letter in your pocket."

Adelle was confused. "What letter?"

"The one I gave you, silly."

Adelle had forgotten all about it. "I didn't realize it was a letter. Is it from you?" she asked as she pulled out the crumpled paper. It didn't look like anything Nora would give her.

"No, it's from Howard."

Adelle rolled her eyes. "What does he want? Another chance to drown me?"

"Just read it." Nora's eyes sparkled.

Adelle opened the paper to see an almost illegible script.

Adelle—I am sorry about what happened at the lake. I didn't mean no harm. I don't want you to think I'm like my Pa. I heard what he did last night. I'm sorry for him too. It's a good thing that guy they grabbed got away.

Howard

"Well, I'll be. I never expected this." Adelle folded up the paper and stuck it back in her pocket. "Thanks, Nora, when did you get this?"

"This morning. He came over, looking very sheepish. That group his dad was with last night—well, they tried to tar and feather a man."

"How horrible."

"I guess last night's rain put an end to that. Sobered them up." Nora looked over at the adults who all seemed to be talking at once. "I think Howard didn't want you to think ill of him."

Adelle shook her head, amazed. People sure could be surprising. If they were staying longer, she and Howard might have been friends, but with Karl coming home she was sure they'd be leaving for Milwaukee soon.

Later that afternoon Mother asked Adelle to accompany her to the lake. They both stood in silence for a time, just gazing on that huge expanse of blue. Seagulls dipped and soared, looking for breakfast. The rain from the night before had cleaned the air, even of the fish odor that Adelle hated.

Then Mother put her arm around Adelle, something she hadn't done in a long while.

"I'm sorry, Addy."

Adelle watched a single tear trickle down Mother's cheek.

Adelle didn't know how to say the words tumbling

around in her head. How to say she understood, that she knew how scared Mother was for Karl, because Adelle had been that scared too. So she just squeezed Mother's hand. They walked back to the house hand in hand, to be greeted by Uncle Mike, his smile a welcoming beacon.

Before entering the house, Adelle looked back at Lake Superior once more. It didn't seem so threatening today. Captain Nemo had wanted to hide under the sea. Adelle had wanted to hide from being German, and all the troubles it meant.

She didn't feel that way any longer. Not after last night. No matter what the future held—or who she had to stand up to—Adelle knew she could be strong and brave.

She knew now that she was proud of her German heritage, and she was proud of being an American, too. It shouldn't matter, she thought, what country someone was born in. It should matter most what they held in their heart, what they knew was true and right.

She thought again about what had happened last night when the angry crowd had come into Uncle Mike's front yard, looking to blame someone for all the things they didn't like in the world. She knew that she had done the right thing. Someone had to stand up to bullies, to stand up when other people were ready to do the wrong thing just because everyone else around them had caught the same foolish fever.

But right now, there was only one question Adelle had.

"Mother, when will we be going back to Milwaukee?"

"Soon as possible, Addy. Our boy is on his way home." Her mother held the door open for her, and they both went in.

Inside, her mother began pouring tea and smiling a kind of smile Adelle hadn't seen in ages.

Adelle had to smile, too. Her mother was calling her Addy again.

And Uncle Mike would have a new fishing partner.

And Karl was coming home.

The End

AUTHOR'S NOTE

What Adelle and her mother did not know was that World War I, otherwise known as the Great War, would soon be over. The armistice, or peace treaty, was signed on November 11, 1918. For many years November 11 was celebrated as Armistice Day. Today that date is known as Veterans Day, a national holiday.

Before peace came, though, the 32nd Division, comprised mostly of men from Wisconsin and Michigan, suffered 14,000 casualties. Known as the "Red Arrow" division, these men were the first to set foot on German soil.

I have taken some liberties with dates and events in this fictional story of a young girl, growing up during the summer of 1918. Two German professors were tarred and feathered in Ashland, Wisconsin, in April 1918. I moved the date to the Fourth of July to serve my story, as I wanted the story to take place during Adelle's summer vacation.

The audience sings the "Star Spangled Banner" at the Fourth of July celebration. This song was not yet the national anthem—that didn't happen until an act of Congress in 1931. However, a similar spontaneous singing of the song really did occur at the World Series of 1918, so such an event surely could have taken place at the park.

A worldwide influenza epidemic occurred in 1918. Many people died, including many soldiers during the war. I mention that Uncle Mike and almost everyone else contracted the flu that spring. Although there is some evidence that the epidemic actually began in the spring of 1918, the most serious outbreak was in the late summer and fall, and in fact did not occur in Ashland until the fall of 1918. Again, I took this liberty with dates to serve my story.

Many years ago my mother told me how, when she was a very young girl, German language books were burned during World War I. Her stories led me to research that time period, and ultimately Adelle's story was born. All of the incidents she mentions in the story involving the persecution of German-Americans are true.

There really was a machine gun set up in Milwaukee in front of the famous Pabst Theatre, because it was a meeting place for the German community. German dances were cancelled. A law was passed that people could not speak out against the war. German language newspapers were confiscated (stolen) by the post office. People were forced into buying war bonds (the money used to help fight the war) even if they could not afford them. It wasn't just German-Americans who suffered. Other groups, such as the Mennonites, were persecuted for their opposition to the war. In time of war, people become frightened. Fear all too often leads to the loss of civil rights.

Growing out of all the abuses, though, came an organization that worked to prevent this type of thing happening again. Today, that organization calls itself the American Civil Liberties Union.

GLOSSARY

Here are some German words used in the book.

Bavaria—The largest state in Germany, located in the southeast. The capital is Munich.

Dirndl—A dress with tight bodice, short sleeves, low neck, and gathered skirt. Traditional dress of Bavaria.

Dummkopf—Literally, "foolish head." Adelle's mother uses it to mean "a foolish person."

Kraut—Literally, "cabbage." Used disparagingly against Germans and German Americans. An insult.

Hun—A derogatory insult used against Germans and German Americans to portray them as bloodthirsty, destructive vandals. The Huns were a tribe who gained control of parts of Europe under Attila, about 450 AD.

Lederhosen—Leather shorts. Men and boys wear these in Bavaria, usually only for special events.

Liebchen—Darling. Adelle's mother uses it to mean loved one.

Mädchen—girl.

READ MORE

Bausum, Ann. *Unraveling Freedom: The Battle for Democracy on the Home Front During World War I.* Excellent book for middle-grade students on the civil-rights abuses that took place during World War I (National Geographic Children's Books, 2010).

Galicich, Anne. *The German Americans* (Chelsea House, 1996). A detailed history of German-American immigrants: their culture, contributions, and struggles. Briefly discusses harassment of the community during World War I.

Gundisch, Karin; translated from German by James Skofield. *How I Became an American* (Cricket Books, 2003). A fictional story, written from the point of view of ten-year-old Johann, an immigrant from Germany to the United States (Ohio) in 1902.

Raum, Elizabeth. *German Immigrants in America: An Interactive History Adventure* (Capstone Press, 2008). With 3 story paths, 46 choices, and 17 endings, this is an entertaining and educational look at the immigrant experience. Covers the civil-rights abuses toward German Americans during World War I.

Silver, Leda. *Tracing Our German Roots* (John Muir Publications, 1994) Covers anti-German prejudice during World War I, contributions to American society, and information on Milwaukee, Wisconsin.

Reynolds, Jeff. *Germany: A to Z* (Children's Press, 2004). A simple alphabetical guide, looking at food, history, traditions, etc. in Germany today.

ABOUT THE AUTHOR

Stephanie Golightly Lowden lives in Madison, Wisconsin, where she is a mother of two children, a member of the Society of Children's Book Authors and Illustrators, and a substitute teacher.

Her previous books include *Time of the Eagle,* a historical novel for middle-grade readers that takes place 200 years ago among the Ojibwe Indians. When smallpox strikes her family's lodge, 13-year-old Autumn Dawn flees into the forest with her little brother, Coyote Boy. The winter trek of Autumn Dawn and Coyote Boy offers a tale of courage and resourcefulness near the shores of Lake Superior. Set in the fur-trade era of the 1700s in the Upper Midwest, when deadly diseases like smallpox were sweeping through native communities, this is the story of one girl's heroism and strong spirit.

Time of the Eagle was a finalist for a Book of the Year Award (sponsored by *ForeWord Magazine*) in the Juvenile Fiction category, and was endorsed by the Council for Indian Education, an intertribal association based in Montana, for the book's positive presentation of native culture and values.

More information on that title is available from the publisher, Blue Horse Books (www.BlueHorseBooks.org).

Stephanie also visits schools and shares her knowledge of writing with students in classroom programs.